BEGGAR'S CHICKEN

STORIES FROM SHANGHAI

ULRICH BAER

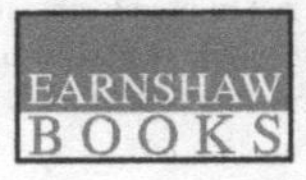

Beggar's Chicken

By Ulrich Baer

ISBN-13: 978-988-16163-6-4

This book has been reset in 10pt Book Antiqua. Spellings and punctuations are left as in the original edition.

HISTORY / Asia / China

EB035

Published by Earnshaw Books Ltd. (Hong Kong)

CONTENTS

Beggar's Chicken 1

Study Abroad 30

Inheritance 90

The Lessons of Tai Chi 130

Control 173

Shanghai Taxi 206

About the Author 236

BEGGAR'S CHICKEN

"Chicken's up!" a gruff cook with a smudged white cap yelled behind the plywood screen separating the kitchen of the *Lou Wai Lou* restaurant from the dining area. In the narrow passageway a group of waiters jostled each other as if trying to board a bus at rush hour. Wen Li, clad in a blue service uniform, reached for a heavy platter. "Taking your time, huh?" the cook snapped through the long window where they passed the food from the kitchen to the wait staff. "Don't make me throw it," he threatened, and shoved the platter toward Wen Li, who quickly grabbed it by its wooden handles.

"Thank you!" the young waiter yelled and loaded the platter onto a wheeled cart that he pushed toward the brightly lit dining room. By the time he had reached a table by the window he slowed down and obsequiously nodded at the seated diners. For a moment he stood there impassively while four waitresses in matching dresses shaded different hues of red arranged dishes, bowls, cups, saucers, and cans of Coke and beer on a table in a way that left a spot in the center free.

Wen Li had been promoted to headwaiter thanks to his skills with razor-sharp knives and his forbearance in dealing with the equally perilous short-tempered cooks from Jiangsu province who thought nothing of flinging a plate of hot food when the waiters were too slow, or forgot their *thank yous*. But his forbearance had a purpose. And right at this moment Wen Li was close to the point during his evening shift where all of that mule-like patience finally bore fruit. With his closely cropped hair, hint of sideburns, and white, long gloves, he waited patiently amidst the chattering tourists who had come to taste the local specialty.

"Beggar's Chicken," he finally announced, and all eyes were directed at the lump of piping hot mud in which a plump hen had been baked all night.

Shortly after arriving in the resort town of HangZhu from his hometown two years ago with a useless high school degree, 80 yuan in his pocket, and the phone number of Mother's cousin scribbled on a piece of paper, Wen Li had started as a bus boy at the restaurant. A few weeks later he had been asked to pick up one of the waiter's shifts, and after that he lobbied the manager relentlessly to be solely responsible for serving Beggar's Chicken. He volunteered for late shifts, scoured the soup station, checked and emptied rodent traps and, his least favorite job, hosed down the greasy floor of the dish room after peak times in summer. His perseverance paid off. The manager placed him on the floor, and eventually the temperamental cooks shouted only his name whenever the dish came up.

"Wen Li, chicken's uuuuup!" they yelled from the kitchen and neither threats nor pleas could keep their shouting down. "Get the chicken NOW!" their voices boomed as they pushed the platter toward the edge where it would drop as surely as the coins that children cast into placid HangZhu Lake from the peaked bridge, unless Wen Li hustled and reached for it in time. But it was not as if there had been serious competition from the other waiters for the job. None of them relished the task of slicing open a bagged chicken from a hot pack of mud while a round of hungry diners watched their every move. When Wen Li had first cut open the hot dish, however, he had seen something from which he could not turn his eye.

"Beggar's Chicken," Wen Li announced solemnly when the waitresses had stepped out of the way. Without a glance at the customers he picked up a small mallet and tapped at the ash-colored pod on the metal dish. When the mud fissured he used his gloved hands to crack open the pod. His hands briefly disappeared into the baked pile and with a kneading, twisting motion like a doctor assisting a birth, he lifted the lumpy bag from the broken pod on to a second, porcelain platter. Wen Li picked up large shears from the cart, leaned his upper body back and, the glistening steel blades suspended in mid-air, halted for a moment.

This was his moment to focus.

"What's he going to do next?" a heavy man with matted-down hair said to a young woman in a silk jacket seated next to him. He smacked his lips while the woman indulgently beheld Wen Li's serious countenance, mistaking the young waiter's pause for a dramatic flourish meant to whet their appetites and justify the restaurant's high prices. Indeed, Wen Li was about to perform a challenging trick.

He closed his eyes, drew in breath through parted lips, and with a single cut, sliced open the bag. When hot steam rushed past Wen Li, the table was instantly enveloped in the chicken's fragrant scent. But for Wen Li the noisy tourists with eyes widened in anticipation, the waitresses lined up like chorus girls, the shouting cooks, the red-faced manager, the bright lights, clanging dishes, noisy fans and chattering crowd all vanished, for a few long, unsounded moments, in the hissing steam.

Gone was the restaurant; gone was the fairy tale, recounted by Wen Li for all diners that understood Chinese, according to which a beggar had served to a traveler a chicken he had hidden between rocks near his puny fire, only for the guest to turn out to be the emperor in disguise who, upon tasting the chicken, promptly appointed the beggar to become the highly paid and honored chef to the court. In the briefest of moments while the diners waited with watering mouths for the steam to clear and to taste this legendary dish, Wen Li found himself transported back in time to a moment he couldn't forget.

He was a schoolboy in his fourth-grade classroom on a spring morning that had been as unseasonably hot as it had been devastating.

"Look! Look!" a girl's scream had pierced the stagnant classroom where students sat hunched over their work. Only her shouting was real to Wen Li's ears now, for this moment that stretched for him into two long days while the diners around the table ogled the stewed chicken.

"Look out the window!" the girl cried out. Wen Li could see her clearly in his mind's eye. That voice! It was the same girl who had brought a mottled black-and-yellow chick to school earlier that fourth-grade spring, and left him speechless when she had chosen him to hold it. He could still feel the tiny bird's rapid heartbeat against his palm. Now that same girl had raced to the classroom window, pointing down.

Quickly other students followed her lead.

"Look at the fence!" another student screamed when he had reached the window.

"Get back in your seats!" Wen Li's geography teacher had shouted in vain. Wen Li had never heard Teacher's voice crack like this. She was a modestly pretty and usually mild-mannered woman whose face was now a tight grimace above her blue cotton jacket and knotted white scarf. The students liked Teacher and were mostly eager to please her. But now they ignored her in a stampede toward the windows.

"Move aside!" Teacher repeated.

"Look! Look! Someone's on the fence!" a boy yelled out.

"Sit down!" Teacher's voice rang in Wen Li's ear. Other students pushed forward so that he could not move. "Get back to your seats!"

"Someone is on the fence!"

"I saw him fall down outside the window!"

"I saw him too!"

The children's shrill voices bounced off the smudged windowpanes and volleyed around Wen Li's head.

"Who has jumped? Who has fallen?" the thoughts raced through Wen Li's head. He pressed his face against the glass. Down in the courtyard a shape hung over the metal fence, as if someone had wanted to keep a heavy sack from touching the dusty ground. But then Wen Li realized it was no sack. It was the body of the school's Headmaster. From its bizarre position on the fence, Wen Li realized with a shock, Headmaster's face stared up at him with wide-open eyes.

"Headmaster Hua!" Wen Li blurted out. "Headmaster Hua jumped!"

Then he bit his lips, stunned by his own words. He had revealed something the other kids had yet to grasp. They stared at Wen Li, suddenly silent. He felt terribly self-conscious and longed to be back at his desk. If he could just sit down and shut up, he thought, maybe this all would turn out not to have happened.

"It's Headmaster Hua!" another student echoed Wen Li in a hushed voice. "Wen Li said that Headmaster Hua jumped from the roof!"

Wen Li felt everyone's eyes on him, and to avoid their stares he looked out of the window again. His gaze plunged down a second time to be met again by Headmaster Hua's wide-open eyes. Wen Li had the strange sensation that the sight landed *inside* of his head with a heavy thud, as if Headmaster Hua had gone straight from the fence, leapt back up through his pupils into a spot just behind his eyes inside his forehead. He couldn't avert his gaze from the dead Headmaster's piercing stare, like a cornered animal staring at a predator. Finally he was able to force his eyes shut. Wen Li felt the sight race through his ten-year old body, as if he had swallowed something still alive, until it landed in his stomach like a punch.

"Get back to your seat," Teacher shouted and pulled at Wen Li's shoulder.

Teacher's hand slipped off and Wen Li jerked back from being suddenly released. He knocked his head into something behind. A cry shot up and Wen Li caught a glimpse of another boy from whose mouth and nose ran blood onto his shirt. Wen Li felt embarrassed and ashamed.

"It wasn't . . ." he began to apologize but then felt a hard slap across his face.

Not fair! This was not fair! His face burned, and Wen Li knew this was not fair! He hadn't meant to hurt anybody! He had wanted nothing more than to get away from the window, get away from all of the kids staring at him, sit down, and be the good student he'd been until that day.

"See how you've hurt him!" Teacher snapped at him.

"I did not do this," Wen Li stammered, "I did *not* do this."

"Get back to your seat!" Teacher shouted, her voice cracking. Teacher had never struck anybody before, and the stunned students scrambled to get away from the windows and from Wen Li, rushing around him as if he had been the cause of this entire scene.

But this had been an accident! Wen Li watched the other students move away from him in bewilderment. Teachers were not allowed to hit! How could he explain? How could he explain that this had nothing to do with him?

"It wasn't my fault . . . ." he began to say but then he saw the furious look on Teacher's face and stopped.

He struggled to get out of Teacher's reach. He wanted to sit down and make everything that had happened un-happen. Make it unhappen, make all of it unhappen, he thought while tears of shame and anger sprang from his eyes.

At his desk, Wen Li pressed his lips together and gingerly felt the back of his head. His fingers were sticky and he wiped them on his pants without looking. Was he bleeding? He wanted to cry at the injustice of being slapped for something he had not meant to do. "It wasn't my fault!" he wanted to shout but instead put his head down quickly when he heard Teacher's voice.

"Write down what I put on the board," she said sternly. Wen Li tried to gather his thoughts but the effort to stop crying made it difficult to think.

Teacher looked in his direction and Wen Li quickly reached under his desk for his notebook. He rubbed his palm across his face from chin to forehead and wiped it on his shorts.

"Did Headmaster Hua look at me?" he thought but his head hurt too much to come up with an answer. Instead he copied down the names of rivers, regions and cities that Teacher was writing on the board.

A short while later another teacher entered the classroom. The two teachers whispered a few words.

"Headmaster has had a terrible accident," Teacher announced without getting up from her desk. "Today you will take recess inside."

"An accident," Wen Li mouthed wordlessly to himself while keeping his head down. That's what it had been, an accident.

Teacher's voice interrupted his thoughts as if he had spoken out loud. "No chattering! Eat your lunch quietly. And do not get up!"

Wen Li picked up a piece of chicken but then put it back in its dish. He thought about explaining to Teacher that it had not been his fault and felt another sob come on. The boy he had knocked into turned to glare in his direction. Wen Li quickly looked away. He felt terrible about hurting the boy and feared his revenge. And Teacher had slapped *him*, as if he had done it on purpose! He had never gotten in trouble in school before.

The boy still looked at him, with a handkerchief pressed to his mouth. *He must know it was not my fault!* Wen Li's head and face hurt. With one chopstick he traced a pattern in the small pool of tears and snot on the wooden desk.

"No talking!" Teacher exclaimed after lunch. Then she sat there and left the students with nothing to do.

A band of sweat trickled down Wen Li's temples while he colored in the front of a notebook. He could not get the thought out of his head that outside, in the yard three stories below, there hung Headmaster Hua's body on the fence.

Finally, the bell rang and Teacher called out.

"All rise!"

Wen Li swayed slightly as if he had just woken up. He felt as if another whole school day had passed, but then the side of his face still hurt where he had been slapped.

"Good afternoon, *Laoshi*!" thirty-six students responded, their thin voices only gathering on the last sound like pigeons scattered into flight before taking off in a single direction.

Then the students moved quickly to the front.

"Go, go, go," Teacher admonished the stragglers.

As soon as the Teacher on schoolyard duty had dismissed them the kids rushed toward the back gate. There the throng funneled into a trickle to pass into the street, right near the spot where Headmaster's body had hit the fence.

Tiny bubbles glistened in the sunlight where someone had spread lime to soak up the blood. Wen Li squinted his eyes to see the dark stains. Was this the spot where Headmaster Hua had been? He was forced past the gate by students pressing from behind.

On the street a few adults stood by the fence. Wen Li slowed down to listen.

"Headmaster's wife and daughter will have to move out of the school's apartment," a woman said and shook her head. "They were such a nice family."

"She is such an attractive woman, it's a pity," another woman added, and it was not clear whether she regretted Headmaster's death or the fact that his family could not stay in official housing.

"Why did he do it in the morning?" a man said and took a drag from his cigarette. "It seems strange to go to work just to jump off the roof."

Another woman put her shopping bag on the ground as if settling in for a longer conversation. "I heard he didn't die until they lifted him off the fence."

"Shush," a woman said but without much conviction. She turned and looked hard at Wen Li. He wiped his nose and stared at the man with the cigarette. Headmaster had come to work to jump? He had not died until they tried to save him? This made no sense to Wen Li.

"Move along, boy, go!" the woman said and waved her hand toward Wen Li. "Nothing for children here to look at. Go on home!"

Briefly, Wen Li thought about correcting them. Headmaster's wife was no longer a wife but now a widow. Probably better not to point out an adult's mistake, Wen Li thought, and kept his mouth shut tight.

* * *

On the day before Headmaster's death, Wen Li had recited a poem at spring convocation. Teacher had chosen his poem from among all of the grades weeks earlier, and Wen Li had spent chilly afternoons memorizing it while staying with Grandmother in the tiny plot of land she cultivated as a garden. He tried to pronounce the lines with the same precision that Headmaster Hua used during morning assembly. Grandmother smiled proudly while he walked up and down the rock-strewn lot. She could not speak proper Mandarin and soon returned to cursing the snails, the crows, the weather, a sister-in-law who had passed away decades ago, the new government that betrayed Chairman's Mao's ideals, and the debris that blew in from the street and obliterated her work. The plot of land was just a strip behind their concrete apartment building, but for Wen Li there was enough space to roam. He helped Grandmother carry pails of sweet-smelling, yellowish water from the basement faucet, careful not to step on the spindly seedlings that Grandmother tended like baby chicks. He had written the poem about this garden, but Teacher had thought it was about something else.

"You show that diligent work will always yield a good harvest," she said in front of the class, even though Wen Li knew that sometimes Grandmother's labors were entirely in vain. Many of the plants withered in spite of careful watering, and once rain had washed away all of her plants and the topsoil to leave just rock-hard ground beneath.

"You find a good balance of the images in each of the lines," Teacher continued. Wen Li remained silent.

On his way to and from school Wen Li practiced

the lines in what he thought was proper Mandarin pronunciation. Most teachers used local dialect in class, even though every morning Headmaster Hua urgently reminded the students to learn proper Chinese.

"Make Teacher and School proud by becoming exemplary speakers," he intoned over the microphone while the students assembled before school.

Wen Li always made sure to stand up front so that he could hear Headmaster clearly. He sounded so learned! Like a voice from a big city, where people studied books and science, and not from the small town where all anyone ever talked about was the price of food and family gossip.

On the day of Spring Convocation, the day before Headmaster Hua had landed on the fence, it had been as hot as an August day. Wen Li's parents had walked him to school, their heads held high with pride that their only child would recite a poem to the entire school. His father had stuck a handkerchief under the collar of his army uniform to soak up the sweat, and as soon as they had found a seat in the stifling auditorium his mother began to fan herself with a piece of cardboard that she had taken from her purse.

Wen Li was eager to recite his poem. He went over the lines again and again in his head, fearful of forgetting them. His father had clipped his hair close to the scalp the night before, and finally Wen Li stood staring out over the audience like a young cadet reporting for his maiden voyage.

"Please listen to Chen Wen Li, who will recite a poem about the fruits of persistent work," Headmaster Hua announced.

Wen Li began.

"Passing under a willow bowing deep in the sun's late light,

I look for stones that will guide us through the next long night."

He paused, cleared his throat, but could not remember the next line. He stared straight ahead without seeing anything. Then he remembered the next word. He started again and without another mistake recited the full poem.

The audience applauded and Wen Li quickly stepped down and took a seat in the front row next to the teachers. He was terribly embarrassed for having forgotten the third line but nobody seemed to mind. Everyone rose to sing *"March of the Volunteers"* and then Headmaster Hua concluded the morning in flawless Mandarin.

"Best wishes for the graduating class! We hope that you will make Teachers, School, and Country proud."

When the students filed out of the auditorium Teacher told Wen Li to wait.

"Headmaster has asked for you to come to his office," she said.

They walked down a long hallway past a walled-in garden filled with spindly ficus trees sporting narrow, rolled-up leaves. Was he in trouble? He wanted to ask Teacher but she walked quickly and he had to hurry to keep up. She did not seem angry, though, and by the time Wen Li reached the small room crammed with two tables staffed by older women near Headmaster's office he felt better. One of the women even smiled at Wen Li when she opened the door to Headmaster's office to let Wen Li step in.

"A poet must write what the poem tells him to write,

not what he knows outside of poetry," Headmaster Hua said from behind a metal desk lined with two rows of neatly stacked papers. He got up, walked around the desk, and stood facing Wen Li.

"You have mastered the traditional forms of poetry like a student headed for university," Headmaster Hua continued. "But sometimes it is necessary to plow the whole field under for new things to grow."

Wen Li stared at a dented corner of the green metal desk. It did not seem that he was in trouble, he noted with relief. But he didn't understand what Headmaster was saying. A small fan whirred in one corner, and different sized river rocks had been placed on the stacks of papers to keep them from blowing away. Headmaster had a nice voice, but this was the first time Wen Li heard it without a microphone. He strained to listen carefully.

"A poet may be called upon to break with tradition, Wen Li. If you invent a new poetic form you will be able to speak to many people," the soft voice now said.

Wen Li still had not looked up. He saw Headmaster's black slacks and scuffed black loafers. "Our country is ready to imagine something new, and poets will be as important as laborers in this effort."

"I am no poet," Wen Li said.

"Study hard," Headmaster said without paying attention to Wen Li's comment. "Study the old forms, and you will enter a good university and change the old ways."

Wen Li was flattered and wanted to please Headmaster. Or at least listen to the nice voice a bit longer, even if he did not understand what it said. Headmaster placed a hand on Wen Li's shoulder.

"You are dismissed," he said but did not remove his hand. Wen Li stood motionless and did not know whether he was expected to leave or to stay still. Then Headmaster passed his hand gently and slowly along the back of Wen Li's head. Headmaster's touch felt good, and Wen Li wanted to lean his head back to make the touch stronger, to feel more. But another part of him wanted to lean forward and bolt.

Headmaster's hand reached Wen Li's ear. Wen Li felt Headmaster's fingers trace his ear and gently rub the earlobe. Wen Li closed his eyes and forgot to breathe for a moment. It felt good, but very strange. He couldn't think very well, and he also could not really figure out where Headmaster's hand was at this point.

He exhaled sharply, coughed, and stepped back very quickly. He knocked his legs hard against the metal desk, turned another direction and in three rapid steps, more run than walk, was by the door.

"You are dismissed," Headmaster blurted out in a tone that sounded as if he were angry and had trouble getting air, but Wen Li was already out of the door.

He scrambled through the secretaries' office and ran down the hallway past the ficus trees. He slowed down only when he had reached the hallway near the entrance. He was embarrassed to have left the office so quickly and tried to regain his breath. Was he going to get into trouble for not properly saying goodbye? Maybe Headmaster's hand had brushed his ear accidentally when Wen Li had moved forward so quickly?

"What did Headmaster say?" Mother and Father eagerly greeted him just inside the school's front doors a minute later.

"You recited the poem very well," Father continued without waiting for a response.

"It was beautiful, Wen Li," Mother joined in. Wen Li could see that they were excited and proud, and he still was trying to regain his breath. He leaned down to rub his leg where it had hit the desk.

"We spoke with *Laoshi*. She said that you could join a program for gifted students. It is a great opportunity."

His parents' eyes shone as brightly as the army decorations on his father's lapel. Wen Li did not respond. He feared that any minute someone would rush down the hallway and punish him for running from Headmaster's office.

"I have to go to class," he muttered and quickly turned to walk up the wide stone stairs while his proud parents headed for the doors.

Headmaster Hua had landed on the fence the following day.

* * *

Outside of the school gate Wen Li now stared at the stains by the fence and knew that Headmaster's wife was now a widow. Wen Li had heard that in the face of something people could not understand they stayed with the familiar forms. For them Headmaster's widow was a wife even with her husband's blood on the ground right in front of them, ringed by little bubbles glistening in the sun.

Should he have heeded Headmaster's encouragement to break with existing forms? Or was the stain on the schoolyard a sign not to follow this advice? While being jostled along the sidewalk outside of the school Wen Li searched within himself.

"It's so sad," he heard one of the women say.

Wen Li thought that he also should feel sad. But he did not know how. He felt nothing in particular, yet even this feeling did not feel very real to him. The sun was hot and the straps on his rucksack cut through his thin shirt into his shoulders. Sweat ran down his temples. He almost had to laugh for a moment and struggled to stop himself. But sad? He did not know what that would feel like.

Wen Li remembered Teacher slapping him. It was not my fault! he thought.

He had reached his street and now climbed the stairs to his family's apartment. His mother stood in the kitchen still in her factory's beige uniform, preparing dinner.

"Headmaster Hua jumped off the school roof today and died," Wen Li said even before he had stepped all the way into the kitchen. Immediately he felt as if he had to laugh again. He fought not to laugh, and looked down.

"We've heard! Don't cry. Do not think about it, Wen Li, it's a sad thing to do," Mother said and turned toward the sink. Wen Li did not know whether Mother meant Headmaster's death or Wen Li thinking about it. Grandmother came into the kitchen and looked at him.

"Did you see Headmaster fall? Did he hit his head?" she asked Wen Li. He glanced at Mother as if waiting for permission to respond. She remained silent.

He did not fall, he jumped, Wen Li wanted to correct Grandmother but kept the thought to himself.

"He fell on the fence by the school garden," Wen Li responded instead. Then he stepped onto the small, unpainted landing outside of his parents' apartment where Father had planned to build, but never completed, an additional room. He squatted on the rough cement floor and waited for the urge to laugh to subside.

"Do your homework," Mother called out from the kitchen through the open door.

"We don't have homework today," Wen Li responded but not loud enough for Mother to hear. Wen Li opened his school bag and looked over the lists of city and district names that he had copied down in school. What made him jump? Wen Li thought and scratched at his leg with a nail he picked up from the floor. Had he died on the fence, or because it was such a high fall? Did people die while they were falling?

"Set the table, Wen Li," Mother interrupted his thoughts. He went inside, set up a small folding table by the door and placed bowls and cups on it.

"Was this the headmaster who spoke at yesterday's ceremonies?" Mother asked while they ate their broth and noodles. "It's just a sad thing to do at school," she continued without waiting for Wen Li's answer.

"And with such a good job," Grandmother said. "It's terrible for his family."

Maybe I should not have run from his office, Wen Li thought but did not say anything. He was glad Mother did not seem to remember that he had been asked to see Headmaster Hua the day before.

"Let's not talk about it anymore," Mother said. "It's not good to dwell on sad things like that."

Several days after Headmaster's death, Wen Li and his classmates queued up outside the school's auditorium. Inside, Headmaster's body was laid out for viewing. In a long line the students entered through double doors decorated with large wheels of paper flowers.

The auditorium was filled with hot, unmoving air. It took a moment for Wen Li's group to adjust their eyes to the faint light. On the auditorium's stage where Wen Li had recited his poem, Headmaster's coffin sat surrounded by more paper flowers.

"Stay with your partner!" Teacher's voice rang out, futilely. Students slowed down in front of the stage to catch a glimpse while the group behind them pushed on. Wen Li, who was tall for his age, bobbed along and peeked over the heads of his classmates at the open bier.

Was he angry? Wen Li thought when he glimpsed Headmaster's face. He didn't look angry – but then Wen Li was forced out of the auditorium by the students behind him. Like crickets escaping from a burst paper bag, the students scattered in the light.

"Did you see his face?" a boy excitedly asked nobody in particular.

"Shush," said two girls behind him, one of them raising her hand.

The boy moved away as if afraid of getting slapped.

"Did you look at his neck?" the boy asked Wen Li when they were out of the girls' earshot.

Wen Li did not respond. Wen Li remembered Headmaster's voice sounding raspy and out of breath the previous day in his office. Then on the fence, with his eyes staring up, Headmaster had looked as if he had tried to say something to Wen Li but couldn't. Had he worn the same expression in his casket? Wen Li could not remember exactly. The fall must have nearly severed the head from the neck, Wen Li thought but then the girls ran up and pushed the boys, and then the bell rang and they ran to line up with their grade.

*　　*　　*

Now it was twelve years later, and Wen Li could recall the sight of Headmaster Hua's body on the fence only when slicing open another piping-hot Beggar's Chicken at the *Lou-Wai-Lou* restaurant. Each night he waited eagerly for the fragrant steam to rush from the bag and momentarily veil his body. Only then would he be back in his fourth grade classroom, staring out the window at the headmaster's face below. Only then could he see the body hanging on the fence and try to understand Headmaster Hua's expression. But now the sight no longer hurt.

"Beggar's Chicken," Wen Li announced to European and American tourists in khaki pants and colored shirts, and to boisterous groups of Chinese visitors where the women wore silk skirts and jackets, and the men, blazers over cuff-linked shirts and loosened ties. With a ceremonious flourish Wen Li unearthed the chicken and lifted the bag from the hot mud on the table. Under the customers' hungry eyes he sliced open the bag and when the steam rushed up the images returned.

Wen Li stretched as long as possible the moment when the images tumbled forth behind the cloud of steam: the body hanging at a funny angle off the fence, and the pointy fenceposts disappearing into the headmaster's neck. He remembered Headmaster's green metal desk, and then Headmaster's grey pants and the worn, black shoes; Headmaster's handsome face above the neat white shirt. In his office? In the coffin?

Wen Li tried to hold on to the images but as the steam dissipated they vanished like the bands of mist over the lake at dawn.

He opened his eyes and with long utensils served a group of four elegant Japanese women around the table. They shrieked with delight when he cut open the bag, and now sat with chopsticks at the ready when he lifted the chicken from its earthen pod.

"Beggar's Chicken," he repeated in the flawless Mandarin that he had practiced in elementary school. "Enjoy our region's signature dish."

"Three chickens ready for pick-up!" the manager's voice rang out over the restaurant's din and like a stinging insect landed sharply in Wen Li's ear. He quickly handed the utensils to a waitress and rushed back his cart. The images from grammar school had vanished completely, and now Wen Li was focused on getting the next chicken dish to another table.

"Three chickens here," the manager shouted and helped Wen load his cart. "Table 7, by the windows, and these two go out to the patio. Hurry up!"

Wen Li quickly turned around and, donning his white gloves on the terrace overlooking the lake, was ready again.

He leaned back like an angler preparing to cast line and, with his eyes shut and his face turned toward the velvety night sky, he sliced the bag holding Beggar's Chicken to glimpse Headmaster's face. The man's eyes and mouth were open as if he were about to say something. Wen Li did not strain too hard to hear but just remained immobile. If he strained to see more he would be left with nothing but the noise of the restaurant, the diners' chatter, and the sound of his breath.

* * *

Wen Li finished his shift just after midnight. He helped the cooks hose down the grimy floors with a high-pressured hose, changed out of his uniform in the staff area, and then sat with them on overturned plastic buckets to smoke. After one cigarette Wen Li used a big stick to submerge his greasy white gloves in a vat filled with boiling water, soap, and vinegar. He clamped a cover on the vat, careful not to burn himself, crammed his jacket in a metal locker, and left the restaurant down a rickety metal staircase attached to the back wall.

Very slowly, Wen Li rode his bicycle along the quiet lake. On one side the asphalt path was divided from the roadway by a low metal fence, a narrow strip of lawn, and a hedge of low shrubs. On the other side no visible line divided water from stone, and the dark surface of the lake gently swayed only a few centimeters below the slick path.

Wen Li turned from the lake and crossed a multi-lane road, deserted at this late hour, and after a few minutes locked his bike to a post in front of a towering KTV parlor pulsating with multi-hued neon. From a vendor who had spread his wares under a torn umbrella he bought apple-flavored cigarettes that turned out to be fake and tasted like it. Past a short row of small restaurants Wen Li slipped into a wood-framed entry and down narrow stairs into a dimly lit bar. Over the pounding music he ordered a whisky.

A short while later Lu Xian, who worked the night shift as a waitress with Wen Li, took the seat next to him and briefly squeezed his hand by way of greeting. She removed a nametag from her red *Lou-Wai-Lou* dress. Then she leaned over to peek in the thick plastic folder of KTV songs on the table. When a few minutes later the DJ called their first number, Wen Li pulled a second metal barstool to the small dance floor and together he and Lu Xian waited to begin.

They sang in perfect harmony of the greatness of their country while on the KTV monitors the winds swept through yellow wheat, raked across sparkling snow on mountain tops, and tousled the hair of laughing youths in front of silver skyscrapers. For the finale two erstwhile stars of old propaganda films shone on the screens, now rotund and enjoying a second career, slowly spun on a glittering stage ringed by a studio audience. Near the song's end, Wen Li and Lu Xian looked into each other's eyes while landing on a plaintive, drawn-out note.

After the final beat the waiters with their spiky hairstyles saluted Wen Li and Lu Xian with staccato blows on the red whistles worn on chains around their necks. Wen Li and Lu Xian resumed their seats and ordered more drinks.

Many times Lu Xian had made it clear to Wen Li that she wanted to make real the intimacy they enacted a few nights a week on the KTV stage with a series of gifts: small envelopes with a pressed good-luck flower in his locker, a little hand-painted tin of tea, a photograph of her with its edges neatly lined with their names in gold and silver pen. Wen Li thanked her for these presents. Then he would find them again, later, in unexpected places: in his old bicycle repair kit; inside the sleeve of a jacket he hadn't worn in months; behind the stove. When they thus appeared, after having been glanced at once but instantly forgotten, he looked at them not quite sure of what they were, and then put them back into another place where they would rest immobile again, like ladybugs after the first cold days until touched by a warm hand.

Wen Li rose to sing a Taiwanese pop star's ballad about unrequited love. Lu Xian pulled her thin scarf a bit tighter and for the catchy refrain slid off her stool to join him. They sang *Wo ai ni* in harmony. Lu Xian sought out Wen Li's eyes to see whether he was just play-acting or whether there was a chance that he believed the words. His voice sounded true. A young couple in love, this is what they looked and sounded like to the few patrons scattered along the walls and the small gang of waiters hovering by the bar.

Wen Li, meanwhile, wondered whether or not Lu Xian would come to his place tonight.

"Ask her to be your steady girlfriend," Mother had urged him on the phone during their weekly calls on Sunday morning.

"With your job and hers you'll be able to save for an apartment," Father had added.

"She's so pretty in the pictures, and sounds nice," Mother had stressed. "Don't wait too long for happiness to find you!"

Wen Li was less sure. He liked the nights with Lu Xian, but to plan for a future together? If she came over tonight, fine – but he wasn't about to ask her out. She did not seem to mind terribly, he thought while she got up to sing another song. And nobody was getting hurt the way it was right now.

I'll let you go, Lu Xian's voice rose with the lyrics that scrolled across the screen above the little black-floored bar.

So – you'll – come – back, she sang along with the colored ball bouncing along the characters on the screen as she looked at Wen Li.

He let himself fall into the next song, for a moment not thinking at all but his mind and body all becoming voice, the way he had sung in the school choir as a boy.

I can be all for you, he sang and his voice soared while Lu Xian stared at him across the dingy bar. He gazed back but did not really see her, instead feeling only his voice all through his body, *all that you lack.*

* * *

Wen Li and Lu Xian walked along the lake and past a festively lit teahouse with no customers. The lakeshore was peaceful and quiet, as if all daytime sounds had settled for the night in the lush treetops along the flat, velvet-black lake. They walked in silence, as if they had already expended all words for the evening in song.

"You okay to come over tonight?" Wen Li asked finally.

"Sure," Lu Xian responded, struggling to conceal the excitement in her voice.

After some twenty minutes they turned into the road leading to Wen Li's home. They slipped unnoticed by a guard dozing in his station into the apartment complex, and Wen Li carried his bike up, careful not to bang into the metal railings and wake the neighbors. There was only a sliver of space between the bed and the wall in his small studio, and Wen Li had to let Lu Xian squeeze past to reach the bathroom door. It was a warm night, and Wen Li closed the shutters but not the glass windows that separated his apartment from the communal landing. With a few plastic clothespins he pinned the curtains to the window frame. He dropped his keys, some coins and bills on a single shelf next to a framed photograph of his father as a young man in military uniform, two smaller pictures of his parents before he was born, and a framed certificate naming him *Grade 4 Student of the Year* in gold characters.

Above the shelf hung a poster of a Taiwanese pop singer with a vacant gaze. It was the same teen idol who had gotten Wen Li to profess his love earlier that night in song. Lu Xian emerged from the bathroom and while Wen Li squeezed into the tiny lavatory she undressed quickly.

Wen Li emerged from the bathroom and got into bed. He slid a leg in between hers, and put his arms around her neck and back. They hugged for a while, Lu Xian's hands on his body and his hands finding her shoulders, neck, then breasts, as if they had started two different songs and only now found the melody. When they made love Wen Li felt his breath getting louder and stronger, filling his whole body with deepening shivers that lastly, with sweat dripping from his forehead into her eyes, also set her off. She was panting and restless afterwards but finally fell asleep, the bedspread bunched next to them, and the pillows half-stripped of their cases.

*　　*　　*

A few hours later Wen Li gently extricated himself from Lu Xian. He covered her with the jungle-themed bedspread, moved the curtains a bit, and sat on the edge of the bed to smoke. He watched the smoke from his cigarette and, in the distance, saw the silvery mist rise from the lake while the sun slowly cleared the mountains behind HangZhu. Bands of yellow skimmed across the surface like glittering snakes until finally the mist lifted and for a moment the whole lake was bathed in a soft orange glow. Wen Li slipped quietly into bed so as not to wake Lu Xian. He gently played with a strand of her hair and began to sing.

He sang the poem he had written and recited for Headmaster Hua at his elementary school convocation, and which he had kept in his heart for all of these years. He sang in hushed tones about walking along a river under weeping willows, and about taking a first step off the shore on to a rock to cross the rushing stream.

STUDY ABROAD

Kevin noticed when he sat down that he had buttoned his shirt the wrong way, one button off all the way to the top where one tip of his collar now jutted out from under his freshly shaven chin. The realization stopped him short just as he blurted out his plea.

"I need your help!" He had put on the cuff-linked dress shirt because he thought it would make him look mature, professional, and with real purpose. Now he put up his hands chest-high so that the director across the desk from him couldn't see the misaligned placket. They were sitting in the director's corner office, filled with a large metal desk, a few chairs and lamps, and framed posters announcing past academic lectures on the walls. Light streamed in through blinds covering the windows, and through two frosted-glass walls stenciled with the crests of Kevin's college back in the US, Kevin glimpsed the outlines of fellow students rushing to class.

"I need you to write me a letter saying I have to be in Shanghai for my studies!" Kevin said with urgency as he leaned forward. "And I need it today."

The director was a large cheerful man who prided himself on knowing most of the students in his program by name, and liked to laugh loudly and often. But at this moment while he was searching for something on his computer his brow was furrowed.

"Your mother sent at least six emails in the last day

or so," the director finally responded, still squinting at the screen. "She's very concerned that you're getting into trouble here, and now you're asking me to help you stay even longer."

"I know that she's written to you, but I'm not getting into trouble," Kevin insisted.

A woman with short hair opened the glass door and stuck her head in. "Your two o'clock is waiting," she said and left the door ajar. The scent of fried rice and eggs wafted into the office from the electric stoves that a trio of women set up daily during the students' lunchtime in the hallway outside.

Dr. Wang ignored the interruption and read from the screen. "'My son is prone to irrational decisions,' your mother writes, 'and I respectfully ask you to stop on our behalf his plans of getting married.' Kevin, how am I going to respond to this?"

"*Prone to irrational decisions*?" the young man blurted out. He got up and closed the door, suddenly conscious that he had raised his voice. "I'm sorry, *Laoshi*. But that's what she said? 'Irrational decisions?' Christ! I'm majoring in finance, I've gotten serious about studying Chinese like they always wanted, and I'm getting good grades. What more do they want? They've been obsessed with me dating a Chinese girl for years, and now that I've finally met somebody they want to stop me from seeing her!"

Surprised by his own vehemence he crossed his arms and lowered his head slightly.

"*Laoshi*, all you have to do is write a one-sentence letter stating that I'm a student here!" he said and looked at the director again. "I can't even believe my mother has written to you about this."

Dr. Wang leaned forward and looked at Kevin.

"Kevin, it's really not for me to get involved in this at all," he said. "But you've been here only for a few months, and maybe it's not the best idea to marry someone you just met."

"I didn't just meet her!" Kevin said defensively. "You know that I met Lin Yi in the first week of the semester, and I will not leave China until I can be sure that we'll be able to be together. Do you know that they will not give her a visa to the US without an official sponsor? She has a master's degree, speaks perfect English, but at the Embassy they still treat her like she's some poor immigrant bound for Chinatown!"

"Hmmm," Dr. Wang went as a way of not responding. He knew the timeline of Kevin's short romance with Lin Yi, and he felt partly responsible. He had hired the young woman to help the American students get settled in Shanghai. She had relieved him of the tedious tasks of resolving the myriad of issues that American students were able to generate, from expired passports to food allergies, and astronomical bills on their American phones until they had learned to get a local contract. Kevin interrupted his thoughts.

"I'm going to marry Lin Yi before the end of the semester, and there's nothing anybody can do about that," he said. "I'm a serious student, and all I need from you, *Laoshi*, is a one-sentence letter stating I'm enrolled in this program."

Without knocking, another student opened the door and wandered into the office, cradling an open laptop in his arm. He looked up from the screen at the two men facing each other across the desk as if they had interrupted *him*, muttered "I'm sorry," and shuffled out again.

"Your mother copied your university at home on this email," the director said. "I'll have to respond to her."

"I am going to marry Lin Yi!" Kevin said defiantly. Although the thought of his mother contacting his college back home didn't surprise him, it made him furious nonetheless. But this wasn't the moment to get angry. He needed the letter, and the director's good will was his only chance.

"I'm sorry, *Laoshi*," Kevin added in a softer voice. "This is hard on me, too. All of this has been a little much, with exams coming up and my parents all in my business, and the tests..."

"What tests?" the director inquired.

"The Chinese government requires all sorts of tests for a marriage license," Kevin said. "You know, health tests. That kind of thing. I've taken most of them, but it takes a long time to get an appointment for each test at the hospital."

"I am not very comfortable signing this letter for you, Kevin," Dr. Wang responded. "Your mother has been quite clear that she disapproves."

Kevin stared at his shoes, his jaw clenched. But he had to show respect to get what he wanted.

"*Laoshi*, please sign the letter. All it has to say is that I'll be a student in the program next semester. I've learned so much in your course about China! And I've checked that I can get my requirements done next semester by staying here. It's just a formality, really." Kevin leaned forward and tried to catch his teacher's eyes.

"When would you plan on doing, I mean, marrying

. . .?" Dr. Wang corrected himself and shook his head over his awkward phrasing.

"Oh, we don't quite know yet. It depends on the Marriage Registration Office. You submit an application, then they notify you, and then you have to come in when they tell you to get the certificate. They may not even look at the letter."

Kevin kept his gaze fixed on the director. If he downplayed the marriage part, he thought, he might get the signed letter.

"I'll have to move out of the dorms right after finals," Kevin continued. "I'll go home to the States and then return for the spring semester. My parents will be fine by then." He noticed the director's skeptical expression.

"I know what you're thinking. Lin Yi wants to get a green card to go to the United States. That's what my parents think, too, and they are completely wrong! Lin Yi doesn't even really like America. She would only leave China to be with me."

Dr. Wang was not so sure. How would an American student understand what America meant to a Chinese girl? How would this boy know what an American green card meant for a single woman in Shanghai? Of course, he couldn't really blame Kevin for falling for Lin Yi. He himself had hired her the day she had walked into his office based on her looks and charm. She had an open face, full and gently curved lips, and she tied her long hair back in a way that made her look at once confident and perfectly at ease. And she certainly knew how to get what she wanted.

Lin Yi had won Dr. Wang's admiration on the day of the students' arrival in Shanghai, in an exchange with a van driver that was as quick as it had been impressive.

"You drive a cab but they shouldn't even let you herd pigs," she had hissed at the man in the Shanghainese dialect which none of the Americans could understand. "You've charged all of these *laowai* twice and you know it! If they don't get their money back right now, I'll make stew out of your balls. Oh, and I'll be sure to garnish it with your taxi license that I'll ask the city to revoke!"

There had been a fierce comeback from the driver, but Lin Yi had stood her ground.

A few of the students started to realize that they had been overcharged. "What's going on?" one of them inquired, but with her best impression of an American smile she dispelled their concern. "Oh, just a misunderstanding," she defended the driver. "He didn't know his company had already gotten paid and refunded your money immediately."

She turned her attention back on the driver and with another choice curse took a signed receipt that would allow her to collect the fares back from the agency. She had saved the students a few yuan. What had impressed Dr. Wang was how she had saved face for the driver while doing so, and kept the freshly arrived *laowai* from getting their first impression of China as a place where you get ripped off.

The episode flashed before Dr. Wang's eyes while he was looking at the neatly dressed student before him. How could this boy know what this remarkable woman wanted? As a bright American kid Kevin undoubtedly would do well in life. He would fulfill his family's immigrant dreams, waltz into some Shanghai company that was sure to give the nod to an American-born Chinese over local candidates, work his way up and, though surely back in the US, start his own business. But he would never understand that it was quite a different matter for the Chinese to succeed in China. Precious few of the American students ever realized that their success, all of the peptalks from kindergarten onwards notwithstanding, stemmed not from pluck, determination, and hard work. They took their position at the top at the expense of native kids who beat them at just about everything but self-assuredness thanks to the location of their birth on the right continent to the right parents at the right time.

"Thanks," the Americans threw out casually, if they acknowledged his efforts at all, when Dr. Wang arranged a coveted internship, got them a private tour of a major company, or set them up for tutoring with a trained Ph.D. Like all Americans, Kevin was naïve about the world, and also arrogant in his faith that if anyone who applied himself sufficiently everything will work out just fine. We shall succeed, the American students had hard-wired into their heads. They could no longer remember in the flesh, even if their parents admonished them to do so, that somebody before them had done the back-breaking work and suffered untold indignities to set them up. They emerged from the customs gate at Pudong airport like overgrown puppies spilling from a cardboard box and, once in China, only rarely realized that they had stumbled into a world with very different rules.

"But if you stay in China there's no reason to get married," Dr. Wang said.

"I want Lin Yi to visit my home," Kevin said, "I want her to understand where I'm from. I've thought about this a lot."

For the first few days Kevin had moved with his friends in a pack that stood out, in this city of millions, like the hulking luxury sedans amidst a sea of Volkswagen taxicabs and bikes. The Americans treated the local Chinese as if they were dull, inferior, and pitiable, even if they dimly knew as Chinese heritage students that these folks held the missing key to their identity.

Upon his arrival in Shanghai, Kevin's Chinese had been the language of a child. He had first learned Mandarin back in the States from Grandma and Aunties but this knowledge was soon swept away by the deluge of English in kindergarten and on television. After elementary school there had simply been no more time for memorizing characters or learning new words for anything not right in front of his eyes. Instead there had been music lessons, later try-outs for the track team, and, finally, all-day tutoring on Saturdays to study for AP classes and prepare for college exams.

One rainy spring day a few weeks into the semester, when flooded intersections halted traffic all across the city, Dr. Wang had been stunned by Kevin's sharply improved language skills.

"Enough rain for the year, *Laoshi*," a deep voice had said behind Dr. Wang while he waited out the downpour in a Western-style coffee shop off Taikang Lu.

He turned around and spotted Kevin, at this point still just one student among many, in a North Face windbreaker and a baseball cap. His face was shiny with water, and the seam of his cap, his jeans and sneakers looked soaked.

"Are you enjoying your tea?" Kevin continued with perfect diction and seemingly unperturbed by being wet.

The director noticed Lin Yi behind Kevin. She was sliding a dripping umbrella into a plastic bag held by one of the coffee shop's young employees.

"Hello, Wang *Laoshi*," she said cheerfully and joined Kevin near his table.

"How are you, Lin Yi?" Dr. Wang responded, "I didn't know you were working today. It's quite miserable to be outside." She wore a slim skirt over black boots, a turtleneck sweater and a fitted woolen jacket with white stitching on the sleeves. Unlike the student she looked as if the rain hadn't even touched her.

"Oh, I'm not working today, *Laoshi*," Lin Yi had responded with an easy smile. She handed Kevin the clear plastic cape and briefly touched his shoulder.

"Yes, of course," he said. It had suddenly hit him that they were a couple. "This is a nice place to stop in for a cup of tea," he added and looked past them toward the café's windows. Kevin and Lin Yi stood by his table as if they expected something else. He continued to look toward the window, not knowing what to say. A man leaned out of an upstairs window next door and struggled to wrap a plastic bag over a handwritten sign.

THERE HAVE BEEN SIX NEW FOOD VENDORS OPENED IN THIS LANE WITHOUT PROPER PERMITS. THIS AREA IS ZONED FOR RESIDENTS AND NOT FOR BUSINESSES -

The wind tore at the sign, and in spite of the man's effort to cover the sign with plastic, most of the characters were already illegible from the pelting rain.

"I really like this neighborhood," Kevin said, as if wishing to contradict the dripping sign that couldn't be seen from where he stood. "It's great how they let the residents continue to live here after opening these little shops. It's much more interesting than Xintiandi. But I hope we are not disturbing you!"

"Not at all, not at all," Dr. Wang said, "I was just catching up on some reading."

How could I have missed the two of them being a couple? he thought. *How long has this been going on?*

"We will let you get back to it, *Laoshi*" Lin Yi interrupted his thoughts.

"It's very nice to see you but you should enjoy your day off," Kevin added graciously, and without even the trace of an accent. And with that they walked to a table on the far side of the café.

The director leafed through the rest of his magazine but could not focus. He worried about their dating. Was it a problem? Was it against the rules? He could not remember whether the rules not to fraternize – that was the word he remembered from a training session at the US college – applied only between teachers and students. The American universities were absurdly strict on this kind of thing, but also petty in defining every aspect of human interactions in terms of roles and titles. Maybe the fact that she wasn't a teacher made it okay.

Although he had not finished the papers and the rain had not let up, he gathered his bag, coat and umbrella, and walked toward the door.

"Have a good day, *Laoshi*," Kevin called from the back.

"I hope the tea has warmed you," Lin Yi added

graciously. Kevin smiled, proud at having her by his side and at the same time self-conscious because he had not understood what she had said.

From the door Dr. Wang saw that the wind had torn the plastic off the handwritten protest sign, which now fluttered in scraps under the small awning, its characters crying ink into the street. The director felt their eyes on him and wondered why this encounter with the student and Lin Yi had left him feeling embarrassed, even though they seemed perfectly at ease. He wrestled open his umbrella in a gust of wind and stepped out into the rain.

That same umbrella now rested in a tall plastic stand near the director's desk in his glass-walled office.

Kevin, still sitting across the desk, pleaded once more.

"The letter only has to state that I'm a student in this program. No different from my class registration but it has to be in Chinese. I sent you the official form so all you have to do is sign."

"I really think you should think about this a bit more," Dr. Wang said while facing his computer. "It's just that you are very young."

He took a sheet from the printer, wishing for a moment that this problem would just go away. He typed a few lines, hit the print button, and handed Kevin the letter.

"Thank you!" Kevin said. "I really, really appreciate it, *Laoshi*, and I'm sorry you've had to deal with my mom."

"As I've said, Kevin, I don't think it's a great idea," Dr. Wang said. "I'll have to write to your mother that I tried to discourage you."

"Thanks, again," Kevin responded, "I gotta get to class!" He quickly gathered his backpack and jacket and left the office.

Dr. Wang leaned back in his chair.

"Mrs. Shangkuan," he typed.

"Your letter raises serious concerns and I respectfully acknowledge the difficulties your son's decisions are creating for you and your family. I've tried to dissuade your son from carrying out his plans, but am afraid that I cannot expel him from the program as you have requested. Since he is an adult we are not at liberty to disclose his records, not even to you. I am very sorry that this is not the information you were looking for . . ."

"Excuse me, *Laoshi*," interrupted the student who had come in earlier.

"... but there is really nothing I can do to end Kevin's stay in China. Sincerely, Dr. Wang."

He hit "send" and turned toward the next student's troubles du jour.

When the email arrived in Kevin's mother's inbox seconds later halfway around the globe, she leapt to action.

"I cannot believe this," she said out loud although there was nobody else in the large room where she was seated at a glass-topped desk. Her slim figure, sheathed to her chin in a cashmere turtleneck dress, was reflected both in the desk's smoky surface and a set of sliding glass doors that led onto a very large and rarely used redwood deck stretching into darkness.

She typed for a bit and then retrieved an alligator-skin wallet from a large, beige Hermès bag on the dining table. Next to it sat an empty yoghurt cup and an open bottle of white wine. Her movements were precise and efficient, and even when she picked up her glass of wine it was as if she was carrying out a task. She typed in numbers from a credit card, hit the return button and dialed a number on the handset of her landline.

"Mom, what are you doing awake at this hour?" Kevin whispered into his phone. He was sitting in a small windowless classroom down the hall from Dr. Wang's office, waiting for his teacher to show up.

"I've booked a ticked and am arriving in Shanghai next Tuesday, Kevin," his mother said and took another sip of wine. "There is no way you're getting married in China! We need to talk this through, and we obviously can't do it long-distance. I've received an email from your director who is very concerned about this whole business for his program. You cannot marry a girl we don't even know."

Kevin got up and walked out of the classroom.

"You're coming to Shanghai?" he said incredulously. "What about your work? What about *Meimei*? The director said he would throw me out?"

"Obviously we need to talk," his mother said. "Maybe you don't realize how upset dad is about your plans. It seems like you don't understand that we're not taking this lightly."

"Mom, it's only a formality," Kevin responded while walking down the stairs of the classroom building. "I'm not screwing up my life, if that's what you think," he added. "I'll stay in school! Lin Yi has already gotten her master's degree and is going to work, but this way we'll be able to stay together."

"Kevin, you're talking about marriage! It's not something you just do without talking to us," his mother said. "I don't know what you're thinking, getting married in China to someone you just met! It's absurd!"

"All you guys ever wanted is for me not to 'lose touch with my heritage!'" Kevin responded and instantly regretted his words. He continued more softly, "Mom, really, it's ridiculous for you to fly around the world to talk me out of something I'm gonna do anyway! The semester is almost over and I'll still be coming home for break."

He stared at his phone when there was no response. "Mom! Mom?" The connection was lost. "Damn," he muttered, snapped the phone shut and raced back to his Chinese class.

* * *

That night, when he and Lin Yi were lying on the single mattress in her cramped room, he cautiously broached the subject.

"My mother called to say that she's coming to visit," he said and stared at the wall.

"Hmmm," Lin Yi said and did not shift her position, hugging his shoulders gently. She waited for him to continue.

"My parents are not happy about our plans of getting married," Kevin finally said and pulled her arms around him. "I've tried to explain to them that we've really thought about this, and that they don't need to worry that I'm giving up my life."

"It's so hypocritical!" he continued in English. "They got married when they were really young!"

Lin Yi played with his hair while he continued to

speak toward the wall.

"I don't want you to feel bad about your parents," she said. "If your mother is upset maybe we should think about this."

"I really love you," he said and turned to kiss her. He rolled over and lifted her on top. He kissed her neck and moved his hands down her sides and to the inside of her thighs. She clasped his shoulders tightly, holding him with a certainty that he hadn't known before. It felt to him as if he were connected to a place for the first time in his life, even if this place was a rock-hard mattress in a cheap apartment identical to thousands, if not millions, like it all over China. With her lying on top, he could feel the mattress under him, and under the mattress, the floor, and under that, many stories down, and reassuringly solid, the earth itself. Afterwards, she pulled the sheets over both of their heads without letting go, and whispered in his ear.

"I really don't want you to get into trouble with your parents."

"I want to be with you, Lin Yi," he responded. "Please don't worry about it. Once they realize that I'm serious about something they are usually okay with it."

She could not know how far this was from the truth, and that Kevin's father had not spoken to him for an entire summer when Kevin had wanted to change his major to film-making.

And not even Kevin could have known how wrong he would be about his mother. Mrs. Shangkuan, on her long flight around the globe to talk sense into her only son, was very far from okay. When she walked out of the customs gate at Pudong Airport past the gauntlet of drivers holding up signs for their respective fares, she spotted Kevin in his hooded sweatshirt and hugged him so tight that he had to gasp for air. He was quite a bit taller than she, and several people stared at the slim and elegantly dressed woman holding on to the college boy for dear life. Or was she holding on to him so that he would not leave? When she pulled away, a slim silver clip and Kevin's baseball cap fell to the floor. Kevin quickly picked up both items.

"I hope you've changed your mind," Mrs. Shangkuan said and put the clip back on her jacket. "Your father said you shouldn't come home if you get married without our approval."

Kevin winced and looked away. "Mom, let's go to the car," he deflected the comment and took her carry-on bag.

She held on to the soft bag.

"I tried calling dad," Kevin said.

"He went to California for work," she said. "And *Meimei* is staying with Aunt Emily. In any case he won't talk to you until you've come to your senses."

He had expected his mother's anger but did not think she would unleash it right there at the airport, where a group of people now gawked at them.

"Mom, let's get to the car first."

"Kevin, you're being ridiculous if you think you'll get our approval."

She pursed her lips and walked in silence next to her grown son out of the terminal. He fended off several offers for a ride and led her to a minivan idling at the center island. The driver jumped out when they approached but Kevin had already opened the hatch and loaded his mother's suitcase.

"At least your Chinese has improved," his mother

remarked drily when Kevin told the driver the name of her hotel.

"I can understand quite a bit but I still make lots of mistakes, and my reading and writing really suck."

He looked over, waiting for a response to what he considered a good argument for a longer stay in China. His mother's eyes had fallen shut. She looked peaceful when asleep, but also older, with her head resting against the doily-covered seatback. He texted Lin Yi, "Moms arrived will call when get 2 hotel," and then closed his eyes for only a moment. Before he could devise a way to change his mother's mind he dozed off as well.

He was startled awake when the car stopped in gridlock on the Nanpu Bridge. The next two days would be dreadful. How was he going to tell his mother about Lin Yi? She would be even more furious once she found out. At least Lin Yi wasn't pregnant, he thought. Not that he would mind, he realized to his own surprise, but was relieved anyways at not having to break that news to his mom.

Some fifteen minutes later Kevin gently touched his mother's shoulder when the van stopped in front of the hotel. "Mom, we're here."

She opened her eyes, looked at him for a moment, and wordlessly climbed out of the van. Kevin paid the driver, handed the suitcase to a bellhop and rushed to catch up with her in the lobby. His mother had handed her blue-and-gold passport to a clerk at the desk and checked her face in a small mirror.

"Don't you want to go up to your room first?" Kevin asked after she had checked in.

"Kevin, I'm starving, and if I go up now I'll fall

asleep right away," she responded.

"There's a pretty good restaurant next door," Kevin said, proud of his growing familiarity with the city that only she could legitimately call home.

In the mall next to the hotel they ascended a series of crowded escalators to the top floor. Kevin was grateful that the bustle rendered any conversation impossible.

As soon as they were seated and handed moist towels, his mother abruptly reversed course.

"Tell me what you see in her?" she asked.

He had braced himself for the storm to be unleashed full force, but not for a heart-to-heart with his mother about Lin Yi. The last time his parents' anger had come down on him, when he'd unsuccessfully tried to convince them he could be the next Ang Lee, it had not relented for weeks.

"Do you think we sacrificed our dreams so that you could end up as a penniless artist?" his father had chastised him. "I'm not interested in hearing how strongly you feel about this. We pay the tuition, and we won't let you waste these years." During these arguments his mother had tried to soften his father's stance. She had taken Kevin's side, reminded his dad of Kevin's good grades, and even looked up how he could get a degree in film and business at the same time. But she had never inquired into his feelings.

"I want to know how you can be so absolutely sure that you love her after knowing her for two months," she now leaned forward to ask.

He had armed himself with proof of his academic success, and with a general argument about growing up, finding his roots in China, making adult choices. Her question caught him off guard.

"What do you like about her?" his mother persisted. "What is it that moved you first?"

"Mom, well, it's not that easy to say . . ." Kevin stalled. He'd never spoken with his mother this way about the girls he'd been interested in. He had answered questions about the neighborhood they lived in, their grades, and, of course, questions mostly about their families. What does the father do? Does the mother work? Does she speak Chinese? Is she on the honor roll? Where is she going to college? They had been through that checklist many times before. But he couldn't remember his mother ever asking how he actually felt about the girls as individuals; whether his heart was involved, and whether it was love.

His mother looked at him quizzically, and he spoke fast to dispel the impression that he didn't know what to say.

"I met her right when we got off the bus from the airport on the first day here. There was some mix-up with the fare or something, and she was just this island of calm in the middle of all of us crazy, over-tired American kids. She just said something to the driver and everything was resolved . . ."

"She must be beautiful," his mother stated. "It can't be that all she did was deal with a cabbie! You speak Mandarin, you've traveled on your own. It must be her looks." She seemed satisfied as if she had solved a riddle.

Then she added, as if remembering her point, "It's certainly no reason to embarrass your parents."

"Mom, yes, she's quite beautiful. People have compared her to Gong Li."

"Gong Li?" his mother asked. "Well, her beauty's

certainly fading."

"It's not about that," Kevin said, searching for a safer topic as if grasping for a pole on a bus that had very suddenly braked.

"I'm just trying to understand you, Kevin. This has all happened very fast, and it's not going to be good for you," she resumed in her serious tone. "Let's eat and I'm sure we'll find a solution."

It was her usual strategy, one that Kevin had never been able to counter: lead him down one line of argument and then, when he had just thought of an answer, switch to a completely different topic without warning.

She handed him the large, laminated menu bursting with color photographs of dozens of dishes. Kevin ordered soup, *xiao long bao*, chicken, and several vegetable dishes.

She must be completely jet-lagged, he thought. *What moved me first?* What kind of question is that?

When he pointed at some images because he did not know the names for the dishes, Mother smiled at the waitress, as if to apologize for him, and continued to order.

"Please tell the chef to make this very spicy," she said to the waitress and pointed at a picture. "Do you have squid?" The waitress jotted down the additions on her pad, tore off a copy and clipped it to their tablecloth.

Mrs. Shangkuan turned back to Kevin. "So she's pretty. What's her background?"

"Mom, she's obviously Chinese. I thought that's what you and dad had always wanted!" Kevin said defiantly. He remembered all too well the night of his senior prom when he had introduced to his parents a beautiful exchange student from Italy. Really quite pretty, as his mother had pointed out the next morning at breakfast, but really a bit foreign, don't you think, and such big teeth.

"Your father and I certainly hadn't wanted for you to get married in college," his mother said and snapped apart her chopsticks. She took a dumpling from a basket the waitress had placed on the table, dipped it in soy sauce and bit off a tiny piece.

"You just cannot get this in the States," she sighed after having chewed for a moment with her eyes closed. "I would make the trip over here just for this."

For a few minutes they ate in silence. Kevin did not know what to say, hoping that his mother was perhaps finished, at least for the moment.

She placed bits and pieces on his plate. "Try this!" she said, and "this is really good," as if she had flown around the world to offer her grown son these morsels in a mall.

"She's an amazing person, Mom," Kevin ventured, emboldened by his mother's apparent pleasure in the food.

"I'm sure she is, darling," Mrs. Shangkuan said as if she had not quite heard him and ladled a piece of double-boiled pork onto his plate. "It's just that that's no reason to get married. Your father offered to put up some money so she can get a visa to come to the States."

"This is not about a visa!" Kevin put his chopsticks down. "Lin Yi has a job. The point is that I want to be with her. I know she's the one for me, Mom!"

"Kevin, I'm sure she's lovely but there's no reason to get married right away. You're a junior in college!

You'll have to graduate and go to graduate school. The heart, Kevin, is no reliable guide."

"Mom, maybe I don't want to go to graduate school right away. My boss said that I could work for his agency full-time after I graduate! He's a really cool guy. I think he's gay but he's been really great to work for."

"They have gay guys in China now? That's certainly something new. Well, Kevin, so you could just come back to Shanghai after you graduate and work here again. That's precisely a reason why you don't need to get married right now! But we can talk about it tomorrow."

Here it was again, the bait-and-switch, when his mother would abruptly change course in a conversation when the argument did not go her way. Although he knew better he tried once more.

"Mom, China is by the far the most interesting place for me. You and dad always wanted me to learn proper Chinese, and at least now I'm making up for that! Lin Yi has lots of friends in the city and we . . ."

"I'm too tired to talk about it now, Kevin."

He bit down hard. They paid and left the restaurant, walking in silence along the mall's half-finished top floor and wound their way down the criss-crossing series of escalators. The last escalator took them down to the vast atrium where throngs of adults and children clustered around food stalls staffed by salespeople in colorful aprons and matching caps who handed out samples while commuters pushed toward the subway entrance nearby. Kevin guided his mother through this candyland of traffic-sign-sized lollipops, pyramids of dried fruit, dumplings, and sweets. Then he realized that the exit they needed to take was a floor above. While passing through the crowds like salmon headed upstream, Kevin's mother's purse snagged on the string of two balloons held by a little boy. The boy stared and jerked with increasing force to free his Mylar tiger and yellow SpongeBob.

"Careful, little man," she smiled while gently detaching the string from her purse's clasp.

But when she and Kevin stood wedged on the escalator going up, she whispered with no humor in her voice, "So spoiled. The children here get anything they want, and they won't know how to work for anything when they grow up. It sure wasn't like this when you were young."

"They're just kids," Kevin said defensively, "it's really no different from how I grew up."

"I don't remember you getting everything you wanted," she said curtly, having the last word yet again.

He wanted to walk ahead quickly, away from her, but he also wanted to show off his knowledge of the new Shanghai. They passed a woman holding a bicycle packed with small wire cages crammed with yellow ducklings and tiny pet rabbits.

"A bunch of kids in our program bought ducklings and kept them in their dorm room," Kevin said, pointing in an effort to change the topic. "They felt sorry for them but then the ducklings started dying."

"Sounds like your program has its share of problems. That's the thing with Americans coming to China and thinking they understand what's going on!" Kevin bit his lips for having said anything at all. Each exchange felt like one step forward, two steps back.

When they reached her hotel he felt worn down, as

if he and not his mother had just stepped off a thirteen-hour flight. "Mom, do you want me to take you up to your room?"

"Kevin, I'll be fine. You should get some sleep yourself. You look exhausted." she replied, her voice now soft with the care that had padded his later childhood years. It was vexing beyond belief, the way her criticisms alternated with no discernible pattern with such gentle care.

"Pick me up tomorrow at ten so I can meet with your program director."

"I can walk you to your room, Mom," he repeated.

"Don't be silly," she gave him a kiss and walked off toward the elevators. "And thank you for finding such a wonderful restaurant!"

* * *

The next morning Kevin arrived at the hotel early. But just when he had dialed the number to her room from a phone in the lobby, having taken a breath in preparation to sound like a crestfallen but reasonable son, his mother appeared next to him.

"Let's leave now so we can walk," she greeted him before he could speak. "I've been up for a while and went to Fuxing Park this morning. I can't believe how nice the park looks! I watched a young woman teach *Tai Chi* next to the old *Shifus* and the ladies doing ballroom dancing. It was strange to see someone so young teach *Tai Chi*! All of her students must have been at least twice her age."

"Why didn't you sleep in?" Kevin said with irritation, unable to keep his tone under control.

He had hoped to have breakfast so they could talk before his mother would meet the program director. "I know a really nice small café that's just opened if you don't want the hotel buffet," he said. "Can't we stop there for coffee and then get a cab?"

"No, I'd rather walk," she said, already heading toward the doors. "And I had a power bar this morning that was left over from the flight. It's obvious you don't care very much right now about what I want, but I would like to walk."

Of course she was still furious. He had hoped, against his better judgment, that the storm would have passed but it was clearly far from over.

"I can't believe there is still room for all these bikes," his mother said while they waited for a gap in the stream of mopeds carrying parents and their school-aged children, old, rusty bikes carrying office workers in suits, and three-wheeled bikes towered with piles of plastic recyclables being pulled by workers wearing blue jackets and caps. They scurried to the island in the middle of the rushing traffic and traversed to the other side when the flow of cars and cabs let off for a moment.

"It seems like everyone's also bought a car in Shanghai now. When I visited here the last time with your grandmother I don't think I saw more than ten cars the first morning."

"It must have been a very different place," Kevin ventured. They passed a block of apartment buildings dwarfed by a gleaming high-rise.

"This is where most of the students live," he pointed to the building's tiled entrance.

"It's amazing they put you in such a nice

neighborhood," his mother retorted. "I guess they charge enough."

He had seen her for all of five minutes this morning, and everything was already his fault.

"*Bu yao, bu yao*," his mother waved away peddlers greeting them with "*Watch Bag Gucci Prada*" on the busy sidewalk. Without slowing down she suddenly grasped Kevin's arm and glanced at his wrist.

"You bought a fake watch?" she said, looking at his large watch. "You really spent money on that? What happened to your other watch?"

"Mom, it was a joke," he said defensively. "We all got fake Rolexes for 15 kuai when we went to Beijing, and mine still works. I still have my other watch."

"I remember when you got your first watch," his mother said. "You were so excited! You must have been eight or nine."

He remembered the scene unhappily. But at least his mother's anger back then had been in his defense. He had come home in tears from school one day when a boy had taken his new watch. The next day his mother met him at the school's gate and asked him to point out the boy. Kevin was mortified when she hissed something at the boy in Chinese and then quickly twisted his wrist, once, sharply. The boy shrieked in surprise and pain and with snot pouring from his nose handed Kevin the watch before running off.

"Make them afraid of you," she had instructed Kevin on their way home. He was mortified by what she had done but also wanted to know what she had said. Instead of responding she showed him how to twist someone's wrist painfully without using much force. He felt as if he had been let in on an ancient trick that would protect him well into the future.

But the memory made him feel stupid about the fake Rolex on his grown-up wrist. His mother's withering gaze made it look not only cheap, but he suddenly felt a bit like a bully, given how he and his friends had laughed while pressuring a street peddler to let them have the watches for only a few yuan.

"I remember that first watch," he said while they continued to make their way down the crowded Shanghai sidewalk. That watch had filled him with awe ever since his mother's fearless intervention.

"Well, it seems like you found a better one now," was her terse response. The sun had broken through the clouds for less than a minute.

* * *

"Mom, we probably have a few minutes to get tea," Kevin tried. He still wanted to talk to her before she would see the Director.

But they continued walking until they arrived at the gate to the French-style villa that housed his study abroad program. A brick path in a fish-bone pattern led into a lush garden.

"Kevin! And this must be your mother. Good morning, Mrs. Shangkuan," a voice called out. Dr. Wang stood before the finely tended lawn and flowerbeds massed with red and pink begonias like a proud host welcoming long-awaited guests.

He extended his hand to greet Mrs. Shangkuan. "You must be tired! It is so very nice to meet you."

But in reality, the director thought while holding his smile, there was nothing nice at all about this meeting.

He looked at the well-dressed woman of the well-fed son who was clearly here to complain. Another parent who took the trouble to fly over here to raise a stink. Another American mother who thought that by paying tuition he would serve as her offspring's nanny, shrink, and travel agent, not to mention confessor, IT specialist, personal loan officer, and butler all rolled into one. He had earned a Ph.D. in Political Science at the University of Washington by analyzing China-US relations from 1949 to Kissinger so that he could become a teacher who could introduce young adults to the world. But his students' parents took *in loco parentis* to mean that their offspring should be sheltered from this world. There were so many things that these students managed to lose! Cell phones, computers, credit cards, and their forbearance as soon as something did not really go their way. And what got smashed, ripped or broken! Plate glass doors in hotels, 300-dollar sweaters, the inflated self-esteem of privileged, suburban-bred young men and women who really knew nothing of themselves.

When a student cried in his office or cheerfully specified the level of medication that kept her from doing so, he wanted to run. They arrived with loads of baggage, as the American expression went that he had always liked, but not all of it could be stored in extra rooms the program had to rent when the first group of Americans had arrived. He did not consider himself the person designated to unpack the rest.

To do that he'd hired Lin Yi. She had saved students from getting arrested by the Chinese police, procured much-needed antidepressants without prescriptions, and two semesters ago shepherded a young woman through ending an unwanted pregnancy that would never be known to her parents in the States. But Lin Yi's principal task was to shelter the director from the students' free-floating American emotions. She spared him from tearful scenes over ill-matched roommates, failed romances, or a student's shocking insight after receiving the grade of B that he might not be as smart, or talented, or gifted as he had been assured by everyone up to this point. Only when parents got involved directly did the messy problems spill from Lin Yi's cozy office, lined with snapshots of students slurping noodles and mugging into the camera on top of the Great Wall, and into the spacious and glass-walled director's suite.

They had reached the door to that suite.

Mrs. Shangkuan turned to her son. "I'll meet you after your class at the hotel," she said and walked into the office.

For a moment Kevin stood by himself in the hallway, worried and unsure where to turn. He walked down the hall, past the two young receptionists who tried to get his attention, and out of the villa's front door.

"Wang *Laoshi*, I implore you. You've got to stop this nonsense," Kevin's mother addressed the director before she had sat down. "China has been good for Kevin but my son is not ready to get married, and I do not want you to sign the letter for him to do so."

"I understand your concern, Mrs. Shangkuan," the director said. Parents should raise their kids properly, he thought, and not leave that job to a professor in college.

"There must be a way not to admit him to the program for next semester," Mrs. Shangkuan suggested. "He could return in the fall rather than the spring, and by then this whole thing will surely have passed."

"I am sorry, Mrs. Shangkuan," he said, but he was feeling sorry only for himself for having to listen to this. "I cannot suspend your son from the program for next semester. It's actually not me who grants admission but his college in the States. And unless there are academic or disciplinary problems we can't just throw him out."

"Wang *Laoshi*," Kevin's mother switched to Chinese. "My son's future will not be in China. He's here to learn Mandarin and get a head start, but he's not here to ruin his chances. A jade stone is useless until it's been polished! If he does not finish his studies he will not have a good life. We are considering not paying his school tuition any longer if he stays."

"Mrs. Shangkuan," Dr. Wang tried to reason. "The program here is part of his college, so if Kevin's tuition is not paid he'll have to withdraw from school altogether."

"There must be a way!" she interjected, looking at him pleadingly.

"I've spoken to him several times after you wrote to me," Dr. Wang responded, trying hard not to show his exasperation. "Kevin is a very mature young man, and he's turned out to be one of our top students here. All he's gotten from me is a letter stating that he'll be enrolled in the spring."

Dr. Wang looked down at the desk to avoid the woman's gaze. She has no clue, he realized. It's obvious that he has not told her.

"I really didn't think they would go ahead with it," he said, cautiously.

"What do you mean?" Mrs. Shangkuan interrupted

him instantly. She understood what he had said, and yet she had to ask.

"What do you mean, 'go ahead with it?'" She stood up and leaned forward, like a cat ready to pounce. "What the hell do you mean?"

Suddenly the floor was not steady below her feet. She placed both hands on the desk to support herself. She knew this sickening feeling. She had experienced it once before, when she had sorted a stack of bills on their kitchen table and discovered that her husband had spent their anniversary not on a business trip to Charlotte, as he had claimed, but in a suite in an Atlantic City hotel a mere hour's drive from their home. She wanted Director Wang to say something else, something that would take away the gut-punched feeling of discovering that the world that she still worked hard to uphold had already collapsed into a heap of scraps.

Dr. Wang's eyes did not meet hers.

"Kevin has not told you?" he tried, hoping against his better knowledge that he was not the messenger of bad news.

"They've already gotten married," Mrs. Shangkuan stated incredulously, no longer as a question, and she sat back down again.

The silence filled the office. After what seemed to him like several minutes the director looked up at Mrs. Shangkuan in her seat across the desk, where her son had pleaded his case only days before. To his surprise, he saw no more anger and hard-boiled determination but instead tears rolling down her face.

"Mrs. Shangkuan, I am very sorry," he ventured. He had not expected this no-nonsense woman to break down and cry. He had braced himself for threats of a lawsuit, and for being shouted at for having neglected his duties. But not for tears.

"They told me after the fact as well," he added softly.

She looked straight at him but did not seem to register his comments.

"I got married very young and worked for years instead of going to college so that we could start a family. Kevin has his whole life ahead of him . . ."

She lowered her eyes self-consciously.

"I am sorry, Wang *Laoshi*," she said more to herself, as if he were not in the room, or did not matter. "I'm sorry we've caused you these problems. It's just that he did not tell me . . ."

She dabbed her eyes with a tissue and made an effort to pull herself together. He looked at her and watched her face regain its previous calmness, like a sitting room that is quickly restored to formal elegance after a rare and improperly raucous event.

"Oh, no, Mrs. Shangkuan, it's not your fault," he ventured. He felt embarrassed for having kept the information of her son's marriage from her for even a few minutes. And now he felt self-conscious at having so brusquely lumped this elegant woman together with all of the other nagging parents. Perhaps by letting Lin Yi handle the students' problems he had somehow triggered this whole mess?

"Well, Wang *Laoshi*," she said more calmly. "Of course this is not your fault. I had hoped my son would tell me before getting married. I had long thought about the day I would meet and welcome his wife, and pick out a dress with her. I want him to be happy."

For a moment her eyes went blank again. She thought back to the time she had found out about her husband's lies, and how hard it had been for her to live on in that world that he had so wantonly destroyed.

She forced a thin smile, gathered herself, and continued.

"Sometimes in life we have to make difficult choices to get ahead," she added. "Kevin had the freedom to wait and try different things. That's why we thought your program would be great for him."

"He's really done well here, otherwise," Dr. Wang said and instantly regretted his words.

"But that is precisely it," came Mrs. Shangkuan's retort. "He's a good student! This marriage thing will mess everything up for him. To get married at 20, when you don't have to . . ."

She dabbed her eyes again and added in a steadier voice, "And it's certainly a surprise to hear that my only son's gotten married from *you*."

"Mrs. Shangkuan, I am sorry –," he began but did not quite know what to apologize for. He had hired Lin Yi; he had failed to notice her and Kevin's relationship; he had not been able to dissuade them from getting married. He had signed the letter they had needed to get married. He had not told her right away of her son's marriage. And worst of all, he'd greeted this elegant and reasonable woman with exasperation when she had arrived this morning, treating her like just another high-strung American parent about to speed-dial her lawyer if things did not go her way. He had done everything to stay clear of this mess but somehow had contributed to making it worse.

"I tried to dissuade Kevin after I received your first

email," he said, omitting the fact that the conversation had lasted only a few minutes. "And the letter is required for a residence permit in China in any case, so I had to give it to him."

"Thank you for your efforts," Mrs. Shangkuan said, quietly.

He was unsure whether her voice was chilly or whether she was just trying to keep it steady. "I know you tried to talk my son out of this, and I appreciate it. Is the girl here today?"

"She took a group of students on a daytrip to Suzhou," Dr. Wang confirmed.

"I remember visiting Suzhou," Mrs. Shangkuan said.

He was eager to change the topic.

"We know the mayor of Suzhou, and he's been willing to let our students tour the new industrial park. May I ask where you are from originally?"

"My father's parents were born near Nanjing," Mrs. Shangkuan replied, distractedly. She allowed herself to think about her first trip to Suzhou with her husband, in the happier times that she now thought of as *before*.

"My parents left soon after 1949 first for Taipei, and then for the States when I was a teenager. I returned for my first visit back once in the mid-nineties with my mother, before Shanghai became what it is today. We also visited Suzhou then. But there was really nothing for us to see in Nanjing."

The director's phone rang and he switched it off without responding.

"My father's parents were also from Nanjing!" he exclaimed in an effort to stay with the neutral topic. "I visit there once a year since they've moved back. It's changed quite a bit."

For a moment they sat in silence.

"Well, if there's anything I can do during your visit, then please let me know," he offered, hoping to make up for his initial brusqueness. To him, Americans, even those born originally in China, had a somewhat artificial expression, as if they were actors in a play bent on spreading mirth. Only when the tears had rinsed away her mask-like American smile, had he begun to see her, and at that moment something had opened up in him as well. Her pain at not having known of her son's marriage did not make him feel bad; instead, he longed to feel something with equal intensity. Perhaps also to feel unhappy, betrayed, or sad but definitely not to feel bored or cynical or annoyed, the way he did almost every morning when he arrived at work. She had sought him out for help, but while sitting in their awkward silence with the chatter of students faintly audible through the glass walls, he realized that perhaps she could help *him* instead.

She was beautiful, even gorgeous. He watched her eyes glistening from the tears while she searched for something in her purse. Her hair, cut in a slightly asymmetrical bob, had a subtle shimmer that looked natural and nothing like the garish, outrageously expensive highlights sported by his wife and her friends this year. But it was mostly her mouth that stopped him short: It seemed perfectly formed to him, and even more so now that a smile seemed to rise upon her lips. Or maybe it was not a smile but something more mysterious. When she spoke she seemed to hesitate ever so slightly, as if deliberating whether she was going to keep her real thoughts to herself. I want to touch her arms, and feel her cool skin, he thought. I want to trace her forehead and hold her face and play with her hair . . .

"Dr. Wang?" she interrupted his thoughts, and it was clear from her voice that she had said it once before. "Excuse me, Dr. Wang? Would you mind showing me where I could get something to eat? I'm afraid I've not had any breakfast, and I feel a bit faint."

"Yes, yes, of course. Absolutely," Dr. Wang stammered. He noticed with embarrassment that looking at her had gotten him excited.

She rose and walked toward the door. He quickly seized the opportunity when her back was turned to get up and smooth down the front of his pants.

They left through the gate. Outside the building a small crowd of passers-by watched a man furiously smash a wicker chair and two wooden footstools to pieces. Dr. Wang gently guided Mrs. Shangkuan along the curb so that no scrap would hit her. For a moment she intently watched the scene but then moved on. The thought that she was alone flashed through his mind, and he quickly caught up to walk alongside her.

A short while later they squeezed into a booth on the second floor of a hotpot restaurant that was starting to fill up with the regular lunch crowd.

"I have to apologize about earlier," Mrs. Shangkuan said. "I must be a bit jet-lagged after all. I just wasn't expecting to find out that they had already gotten married. It's certainly not the way I would have hoped to find out."

He did not know whether she wanted to continue talking about it. But she spoke next. "You're very kind to take me to lunch, and I'm sure that when I see my son this afternoon I'll be able to figure out a way to resolve this situation."

"There's probably something we can do," he said.

She glanced at him skeptically for a moment. Then she turned her attention to the ribbons of beefs and sliced lamb piled on small trays and shiny plates. Fragrant steam rose from the broth in the pot sunk into the tabletop between them.

"I think that my husband and I, as Kevin's parents, will find a way to annul the marriage," she said, articulating each word carefully. Her voice sounded colder than before. Then she delicately slid a small portion of cubed meat into the broth with her chopsticks.

"Mrs. Shangkuan, I'm very sorry that I couldn't stop this from happening. Kevin is one of our best students."

Sweat had formed on his forehead, and he twisted his shoulders as he struggled to remove his blazer. He longed for a beer, but was worried she might disapprove of someone drinking alcohol during the day. Even Chinese-born Americans had become prudish that way, something which he had learned in an uncomfortable exchange with a mother who had expected him to keep her college-age daughter from touching any liquor while in China.

She laughed when she dropped a piece of meat on the table. "I guess I've lost my touch with chopsticks," she said with that enigmatic smile fluttering around her lips. "My mother would be horrified!"

They ate in silence for a few minutes, concentrating on placing food in the hotpot and removing it in time.

"Yours is the kind of program where I would

have wanted to study," Mrs. Shangkuan resumed the conversation. "For Kevin to be able to live in Shanghai while he's in college! My parents were not in favor of me studying in China, and I did not have the means to study until my late 20s, so I never had that chance. Kevin has been able to learn so much here."

He was relieved that she was talking, and that she enjoyed the food. He chatted about Shanghai's real estate, and volunteered a few innocuous anecdotes about air travel. While she decided which food to slide into the hotpot next, he stole glances of her.

"There's no place like this anywhere in the States," she said. "It's funny that so many people just come in here for a quick lunch, when you could spend hours eating this delicious food."

"I am glad you like it," he said.

He wondered if she noticed that he kept refilling her glass from the water pitcher; that he was steering the choicest pieces of meat toward her side of the broth. Though he wasn't sure that would matter – after all, what would this wealthy and beautiful woman, who had spent most of her life in the US, see in someone like him?

But there was something in the way she glanced at him, the gentle way in which she touched his arm when she asked him to pass her a napkin and so he made sure to hold his head and shoulders high as they left the restaurant and – just in case, when she wasn't looking – he tucked his shirt in so that his paunch would not show.

"I think I'll walk," she said just at the moment he had hailed a cab. The driver stared at them blankly, with him holding the door and her looking every part the spoiled and capricious Shanghai wife who could not make up her mind. When she did not say anything he shut the door, and the driver sped through the red light as if making up for lost time.

"I will be happy to walk you to your hotel," Dr. Wang said. He felt a bit giddy, as if he had just downed a double espresso, or the way he had felt as a boy when his father handed him the line to a fantastically large yellow and gold kite with long streaming tails soaring above them in the autumn sky.

*　*　*

"I am so sorry, Mom. I really was going to tell you today," Kevin pleaded for the third time. She had not said a single word after letting him into her hotel room several hours before. Kevin sat on the bed's copper-colored comforter while his mother sat with her feet curled under her on an over-sized chair by the window.

Her hands gripped the arms of the chair while he repeated his apologies, and as she stared past him, focusing blankly on the wall, the strain on her elegant hands was the only part of her that betrayed any emotion.

"Mom, I thought you were too tired yesterday, and there wasn't really any opportunity this morning for me to bring it up," he said.

"I cannot believe that you did not tell me or your father that you had gotten married. You told that program director before us!" she finally hurled at him. Her tone was so sharp Kevin felt like he had been slapped in the face, and the next moment he was awash in a torrent of guilt and failed expectations.

"Did you expect us just to approve of this after the fact? Did you? Why did you even bother to tell us about your plans in the first place? You have disgraced your family! To marry without your parents' approval, and then to tell other people about it before we had a chance to find out! This is not how a son behaves if he wants to make his parents proud." She turned her head toward the windows, as if looking at him caused her pain. "We did not raise you this way!"

The sentence hung in the air as if she had sliced through it with a sword.

She turned her head, resting her chin in the palm of her left hand.

"I am so sorry," Kevin ventured shakily. "I know it was a huge mistake not to tell you beforehand."

"It was a huge mistake not to talk to us about it beforehand. The fact that you got married at all, without our approval is so disrespectful, so disgusting!" she cut in. "You're sorry! You're sorry! Of course you're sorry now, when it's too late." Her voice pitched into sarcasm. "What would you like me to say? What do you think your father will say? Oh, it's okay, Kevin, since we can't change anything now we'll just go along with it?"

"Mom, I am truly sorry. Really." He tensed up his shoulders. "It's just that it's so difficult to get an appointment with the Chinese authorities. We got the notice very suddenly and if we hadn't accepted it we probably would have waited for another year. I thought that with you flying over here and everything it would be easier to tell you in person."

"Well, Dr. Wang was the one who told me. He is the only person who has been honest with me so far," his mother said sharply. "I cried in his office. I cried in front of a complete stranger! My only son gets married and I have to hear it from someone I have never met before."

Kevin bit his lip and looked down at the floor.

"You have no idea what you have done, Kevin! You're too young to tie yourself down! You have so many things you can do! You have opportunities."

The last words had sounded more regretful than angry. She took a breath and then sighed.

"Today people don't have to get married so young. I had looked forward to meeting the girl you would marry in the proper way."

A chime at the door interrupted them.

"Go answer it," she said, sounding tired. A waiter wheeled in a cart laden with two place settings, a vase packed tightly with tiny-blossomed yellow roses, and several silver-topped dishes.

"You like me serve?" the waiter asked in halting English. His nametag read "Sugar" as an English approximation of his Chinese name. He was close to Kevin's age but skinnier, and looked almost gaunt in the black hotel uniform. Kevin felt self-conscious next to this unexpected doppelganger. His mother watched impassively while Kevin explained in Mandarin to the waiter that he had come to the wrong room and showed him out.

"Mom, I wanted you to meet her in the proper way too. It all just happened so fast. You go to a city clerk, they look at a lot of paperwork and then you sign the forms," Kevin ventured again. "I would have told you but we did not find out about the appointment until the day before. It's the only way we can be together."

"Kevin, you cannot just follow your heart! To follow your heart means to lose your way. Your father and I worked hard to build this life so that it won't suddenly collapse. If we had followed every whim –" She cut herself off. If she had followed her heart when she was Kevin's age, Kevin would not be sitting in front of her right now.

"But you and dad have always said you want me to be happy," Kevin responded tentatively. He sensed that her thoughts had taken her elsewhere, and did not know what would follow next.

"Happiness is what you can plan for, Kevin!" his mother retorted. "It's not doing whatever you feel like at the moment."

"Mom, I am not dropping out of school," Kevin said. "I would have asked you but I thought we could have another ceremony later on. Lin Yi will work, and so we'll start out the same way you and dad did."

"But this is precisely the difference, Kevin! Your father and I *had* no choice but to start out this way!" She quickly caught herself, as if surprised by her own words. "Kevin, for you it's different. You're an American and you have the whole world within your reach, ready for you to explore. Your father and I got married young and worked hard so that you could plan your own life."

Kevin remembered his parents' anger when he had wanted to change his major to film.

"First you say nothing in life is certain, Mom, and now you say I should explore the world." He was no longer apologetic, but defensive, and now decided rashly to go in for the strike. "You and dad got married very young because you had to, but for Lin Yi and me it's because we're in love –"

"I am not having this discussion," his mother cut him off sharply before he could continue. "You're too young to know what you're doing, you've known this woman for three months at most, and she's probably interested in you mostly because you can get her a green card."

"This is not it," Kevin blurted out but retreated quickly.

"What prompted you to do this?" his mother said, in a softer tone. "You said she's not pregnant and she has a job. You could have continued to see each other without getting married. We can put money in an account so she can get a visa. What is it that you see in her? Does she make you happy?"

Kevin did not want to respond although he was sure, yes, absolutely certain, of the answer.

His mother looked at him probingly.

"She makes me very happy," he said slowly. He did not add that he could not get enough of Lin Yi, and that he thought about little else during the day but the time when he could finally see her alone at night.

"What is it about her then?" his mother asked again.

Kevin was contrite but he did not trust her sudden change in tone. His mother was liable to flip any of his comments on their head and make him feel inadequate. Let her be furious, he thought, but I will not let her question my love for Lin Yi.

"I am trying to understand you, Kevin," his mother said.

"Lin Yi is a wonderful person," he continued in a deliberately even voice. "She's smart, sophisticated, and charming." As if I'm writing an on-line ad, he thought. As if those were the reasons that made me fall for her.

"Kevin, there must be something else," his mother tried in a gentler voice as if she could read his mind. "I just want to find out what has prompted you to listen to your heart."

He realized that she wanted an answer to this question because it concerned not only him but *her*, and he sensed that by answering honestly he wouldn't win this battle but somehow have her on his side.

* * *

There was a dinner that night at the *Lost Heaven* restaurant in the French Concession. Only a day before Dr. Wang had tried to get out of this dinner. But now, after this morning's meeting and lunch, he had taken care to put on a fresh shirt and made sure to arrive early.

Kevin had left his mother to rest for a bit. When he picked her up she looked quite composed, in black slacks and a muted charcoal silk jacket. They arrived at the restaurant and entered through tall, carved doors salvaged from a temple in Yunnan. They passed a bevy of crimson-clad hostesses and entered the lounge area on the first floor. Lin Yi, who had been standing at the bar, quickly handed her diet coke to a waitress and hurried to greet them.

She was sheathed in a grey thin shift over grey leggings and a dark green cotton scarf. She extended her hand to greet her mother-in-law for the first time. "Let me look at you," Mrs. Shangkuan clasped the younger woman's two hands.

Dr. Wang watched them intently from the bar. "She must have been drinking to be so calm," he thought, remembering the emotional scene in his office earlier that day.

But Mrs. Shangkuan was perfectly sober.

"This is certainly not the way I thought I'd meet my daughter-in-law," she said to Lin Yi, "but my son has convinced me that he knows what he is doing."

Kevin smiled awkwardly and raised his eyebrows. He did not trust the scene, did not trust his mother being nice. This was going to explode anytime now, and he could not understand why his mother had insisted on meeting in such a public place and with the director there, too.

Lin Yi paid him no mind. "I apologize for not waiting for your approval, Mrs. Shangkuan," she said graciously.

"I must say my son has exquisite taste," Mrs. Shangkuan said, looking straight at Lin Yi. Kevin, standing by her side, awkwardly realized that this quick mutual appraisal by the two women in his life, their eyes fixed on each other without so much as a glance at him, was just the beginning. He tried unsuccessfully to catch Lin Yi's gaze. His mother held the younger woman's wrists as if she could read her character by touch alone. Lin Yi looked comfortable, even relaxed, and with open eyes she held Mrs. Shangkuan's gaze the way you afford a fortune-teller a good look so they get a better read.

"Kevin's told me a lot about you," Mrs. Shangkuan said to Lin Yi. "And about the way you've encouraged him to become serious about his studies of Chinese, and how you've applied yourself to your career. I've not known him to be this serious about anything else in his life."

Kevin held his breath.

"You know that my husband and I had been worried about him," his mother continued. "He did not seem very focused on his studies before he went to China, and wasn't even sure about what to study. It seems that being in Shanghai has really changed that."

This is way awkward, Kevin thought. His mother talked about him as if he wasn't even there, or, worse yet, as if were in grade school and Lin Yi his teacher. Looking around at Lin Yi and Director Wang, though, he realized that he was the only person who felt uncomfortable.

"All of Kevin's motivation clearly comes from you and your husband," Lin Yi agreed with Mrs. Shangkuan. "He's told me about you attending college when he started first grade, and getting a master's degree while working when he was in high school."

"Oh," Mrs. Shangkuan looked at her with surprise and glanced at Kevin, "I never knew he appreciated any of that!"

"It's okay to speak English," she finally told Lin Yi as if the formal part of the introductions were over now.

"Our son certainly has not made this easy on us," she said and cast a quick look at Kevin. Lin Yi squeezed her lips and bowed her head, Kevin noticed to his astonishment, as if she agreed. He again tried to catch her eye, feeling like a waiter trying to get the attention of an important diner without wishing to interrupt the conversation.

"Kevin has assured me that he will take summer courses to complete his pre-med requirements. And that he'll learn proper Chinese, something he never did in all of his language courses when he was little!" She smiled and finally let go off Lin Yi's hands. Kevin did not feel relieved. "We would like to host a proper banquet for you when you visit," she added.

"We would be so honored," Lin Yi said in Chinese.

Kevin assumed that Lin Yi's formal phrasing was a way of showing respect. But he felt left out since he had to guess at the complete meaning of her reply.

A hostess interrupted the small group and ushered them to a table upstairs. The large and crowded space was filled with oversized bronze vases, stone urns, and heavy wooden tables lined with high-backed carved chairs. The whole place looked vaguely tropical, overdone, and with the ceiling fans slowly churning the air-conditioned air, like a movie set for scenes that would most likely end up on the cutting room floor. Kevin took a seat next to Lin Yi, their face aglow in flickering reds and purples from lamps veiled by colored silk.

"The restaurant's owner has just returned from Yunnan province where he finds recipes," Dr. Wang informed the group. "He trekked several days through the jungle to taste a special dish in a tiny village of the Miao people. They held an elaborate ceremony where elders cut thin slices of meat for their honored guest."

"Can we order it?" Mrs. Shangkuan asked but Dr. Wang shook his head.

"He said it was disgusting," he said and laughed. "Bland and revolting all at once. He'd spent several weeks and thousands of yuan to reach this particular village, bribing first the officials and then the locals, and then they served him fermented pork that was inedible!"

Kevin's mother and Lin Yi also laughed, and Kevin wondered again whether he had failed to understand something, but he joined in anyway, even if he still didn't trust the easygoing mood. Dr. Wang smiled, evidently pleased that the women found him witty.

"Everything else on the menu was worth traveling for," he continued. "Most dishes come from the Bai and Miao ethnic groups. You really can't find this kind of cooking anywhere else. I think some of it is also from Burma."

"I would love to visit Yunnan," Mrs. Shangkuan said and looked at Dr. Wang with a smile.

A waitress lifted the hammered brass lids off the plates, and Lin Yi first served Kevin's mother. She laughed again at one of Lin Yi's remarks, and again Kevin failed to grasp the reason of her mirth. They had switched back to Mandarin but nobody slowed down so that he could understand more easily.

Under the table Lin Yi put her hand on his thigh. Her touch tickled but he wanted to feel her and immediately locked his fingers with hers. He looked at his mother and wondered whether she had noticed.

Mrs. Shangkuan sipped her drink. "How long does it take to get to Yunnan from Shanghai?" she asked Dr. Wang and chose a piece of meat from a leaf-lined narrow platter in front of him.

"It's not difficult to fly there," Dr. Wang responded. "And once there it's truly magical to travel. I've visited twice and would love to go back."

The restaurant's owner walked up to their table. He looked as if he had returned from the jungles of Yunnan this very minute, in a black t-shirt and khaki cargo pants, and his dark hair glistening as if from a downpour though it had been dry in Shanghai all day. On his wrist he wore a thick, black diving watch and a braided copper bracelet that glowed in the diffuse light. He greeted Dr. Wang cheerfully, and said something to Kevin's mother. She smiled and then raised her eyes up at him without lifting her head. Kevin noted with consternation that her coy gesture had turned the two men into fawning admirers. She laughed, cocked her head lightly to one side and brushed her hair back with one hand.

The restaurant owner signaled a waitress who brought more dishes. He briefly placed his hand on Mrs. Shangkuan's arm.

"Do come back before you leave Shanghai," he urged her and bowed in the direction of Lin Yi and Kevin before turning to another table. Mrs. Shangkuan took another sip of her drink. She felt light-headed and had to laugh again, even though nobody had said anything. The food was absolutely delicious! And these drinks . . . she did not remember anyone ordering drinks. She resolved to enjoy at least this part of her visit and decide what to do about the marriage later. The food was spicy, and she took another sip from the drink.

Under the table her knee was very close to Dr. Wang's thigh. She did not pull back lest he become aware that their legs had been almost touching all this time. She might as well enjoy herself! Kevin had not had any serious girlfriends in high school, and even in college he had spent so much of his time by himself. Of course this marriage was a silly idea. But he had followed his heart, and there was something to be said for that.

She remembered the American boy who had been interested in her in high school. Her parents had not approved. She had pleaded in tearful scenes but her father forbade her to see him. "American boys will never respect your culture," her mother had said, and her father had refused to shake the boy's hand when he had picked her up one night. He had stood at the door with his hand extended, waiting, and her father had glared at him wordlessly for a moment before turning around to walk back into the den. A few weeks later the relationship ended, and that whole summer she had obsessed to figure out whose fault it had been. A year later she married Kevin's father, a Chinese-born college student who'd grown up in the same town, and Kevin was by then already on his way.

She glanced at her watch. Back in the States her husband was probably just now waking up in his apartment in the city that he used during the week. He would be going through a morning routine of which she had not been a part for years. Whether someone picked out his tie, prepared tea, or kissed him before he headed to the office – weekday mornings were his business alone. She had never fully recovered from the shock of finding out about his weekend in Atlantic City, and from his cold refusal to mend things, or to speak with her at all. The recent lunch where they had discussed, at her insistence, what to do about Kevin in China had been a rare moment of closeness, forced upon them by their son's refusal to follow their rules.

"He'll get over it," her husband had said about Kevin's marriage plans and signaled for the check. He wore a tie that she had not seen before, and he seemed annoyed at the disruption to his workday routine.

"Maybe she needs money, or she's pregnant," he had continued. "I'll try calling him but you should tell him that we'll do anything to make him come to his senses."

We'll do anything, she had repeated in her mind, although the two of them had not done anything together in many years. So she had flown to China alone.

The thoughts of her husband wiped away her giddiness. She excused herself and went to the restroom.

My son will get hurt, she thought while squeezing past guests waiting for a table in a long hallway. But at least it will not have been me who ruined his life. She found an empty stall and locked the door. I've tried my best, she said to herself. She sat on the toilet for a few long moments with her forehead against the cool polished concrete wall. Then she pulled herself together. It will not be me who ruins Kevin's life, she thought and clenched her teeth. And I will not let his father do that, either. Let the boy make his own mistakes.

She finished and adjusted her clothes. His father had not thought it was necessary to fly to Shanghai. And he had been right! Kevin's married already! She let out a little pearly laugh and exited the stall.

Everything was bathed in soothing, amber light, and she waved her hands for a moment before the water turned on. She washed her hands over the deep, coffin-like sink lined with smooth pebbles. When she raised her head she looked not into a mirror, as she had expected, but directly into her son's face. He was washing his hands on the other side of the same concrete sink that was divided in the middle by nothing but a floating shelf.

"Mom!" he said, surprised. He looked around to make sure he had not walked in through the wrong door. "I didn't realize that this is a shared bathroom."

His mother looked at him as if trying to remember what she had wanted to say.

"Lin Yi is very nice," she said matter-of-factly. "Well, I made a conscious effort to enjoy this dinner," she added and smiled at Kevin.

"Are you alright?" he asked. His mother's cheeks were flushed and she smiled broadly.

"Don't worry about me," she said cheerfully. She looked at Kevin while she took a neatly folded cloth towel from the shelf between them. He looks so grown up, she thought, and found that insight very funny. He is a man, and he will make the mistakes all men make. She let out a small and bubbly laugh.

"You make your own decisions, that much you've made quite clear," she said to him. "By the way, your father did not think you would go through with it. He thought it was a waste of money for me to fly over here."

There was that same edge to her voice that he had heard for the first time this afternoon. It cut deeper than any of the criticisms she had thrown at him before.

She walked out of the bathroom and he quickly wiped his hands on his khakis and followed.

Mrs. Shangkuan crossed the busy dining room and let herself fall on to the softly cushioned chair with a smile. "The bathrooms are very modern, they're for both women and men!" she reported, "I ran into Kevin!

I guess the new China is going back to communal latrines."

She laughed at her own joke and took another sip from her drink.

"May we get dessert?" she asked. "I'm craving something sweet."

Her son gave her a strange look. It seemed to her as if he and Lin Yi were not seated at the same table but quite far away. Only Dr. Wang seemed very close, and she liked that. I'm not drunk, she thought to herself. She mumbled the same thought to herself when they left the restaurant a little while later. I know what I'm doing. Then Kevin and Lin Yi stood with her by the curb, with the girl gently holding her arm, and her son asking, several times, "Are you okay, mom? Are you sure you're okay?"

"I'm perfectly fine," she had responded in a voice that had sounded clear and sober to her. Then her son and the pretty girl were gone. His wife! She thought and laughed again. One Shangkuan man leaves his marriage without so much as telling me, and the other one enters into marriage head over heels. And also without telling me! She laughed again, and in the empty street it sounded like pearls scattering on a stone floor. Then she turned to Dr. Wang and repeated what she had said earlier that day, right after the hotpot lunch that seemed to have occurred several days ago.

"I'd prefer to walk to my hotel," she said and stepped off the curb to let a young, long-haired man and a middle-aged, well-dressed woman pass. She followed them with her gaze, seeing in them herself and her son until she noticed that they were holding hands.

"We can walk along Fuxing Lu," Dr. Wang said. "Sometimes at night you can hear the music students practice at the conservatory. They are very talented."

"Isn't everybody in China talented?" she responded cheerfully and walked ahead. He caught up with her and gently steered her back on to the sidewalk. They walked under a canopy of branches with shiny green leaves. It was only a few minutes before ten o'clock but the street was deserted. They passed the same woman with the younger man again, now engaged in a hushed conversation in the shadowy vestibule before a store, and with the woman's arms draped around the man.

A bit further down a few vibrant chords of a Brahms quartet leapt over the brick walls of the music conservatory. She stopped to listen, and swayed slightly. In order to steady her Dr. Wang put his hand against her jacket, just below the shoulders. She leaned back into the support he offered, and let herself go a bit more. For a very brief second, really only for one blink, she closed her eyes. He took one quick, dance-like step to gain better footing as she leaned her body fully into his. She could feel his torso against her back, his slight paunch, and his thighs against her behind. She felt his chin against her hair and moved her head a bit to feel more. His hands rested lightly on her hips. When she turned her head a little his lips grazed her left cheek. He moved his left hand to rest very lightly on the side of her face, and she didn't know whether he had turned her face with his hand or whether she had sought out the kiss.

The music floated over the conservatory's walls and although it was soft she could feel it in her limbs and torso. She also felt Dr. Wang's presence but chose not to let this feeling become a conscious thought. It was so good to lean against someone and rest for just a moment!

She looked up at the branches with their shiny, dark-green leaves above, and then along the quiet street. There was nobody else in sight. She laughed briefly and then sniffled, as if she had shed a tear. His hand softly encircled her upper arm and after a few more minutes they separated as gently as they had begun this embrace and walked in silence down the sidewalk past the conservatory.

Just before the corner of Huaihai Road a gold-colored cab spotted them and the driver quickly turned around to pick them up.

In the backseat he glanced at her questioningly.

"Would you like me to take you to your hotel?" he asked and she nodded before leaning back her head.

"Follow your heart," she whispered with closed eyes and placed her hand on his arm. She did not respond when he asked her to repeat what she had said.

In her hotel lobby she searched in her purse for a key card to operate the elevator. Before inserting the card she looked at him directly for the first time since they had listened to the Brahms, and she had felt his lips.

"Would you like to come up for a cup of tea?"

Instead of responding he stepped with her into the elevator. The doors closed and they kissed at once so gently and so forcefully as if they had waited for each other for a long, long time.

To be met in his desire! he thought. The girls at the massage parlors with their skinny fingers and listless expressions had never satisfied him. Those visits were like washing by a zinc basin filled with cold water, next to hordes of other sweaty, grunting men vying for a bit of space. With this woman he felt as if he was lowering himself into a warm and wonderfully scented bath. His lips found her mouth, and her neck and ears. When they were in the room she closed her eyes and relaxed. Then slowly his hands began to undress her, first the silk jacket, then her blouse untucked from the pants, her belt, pants sliding quietly to the floor. She stopped his hands when he reached around for her bra and went into the bathroom.

When she returned he sat on the bed, still in his pants but now only in his undershirt. The lights were dimmed and on the stereo the violins sweetly soared under the lilting voice of Cai Qin.

She settled on the bed and then closed her eyes. She felt how his hands sought the fasteners and undid her bra with growing confidence. Then his hands detached for a moment and she knew, with a certainty that made her swallow hard, that he was pulling off his undershirt and pants.

She slipped under the covers and he kissed her shoulders, her breasts, her stomach and then turned her on her side, and rested his face against her stomach and then moved his head lower. She opened her legs and pulled up her knees a bit. She felt the gentle rhythm of his lips and tongue and swayed with him until his rhythms were eclipsed by a stronger tide inside of her. Its tremors welled first up to her back and shoulders and then coursed through her entire body until her legs and hands were trembling. She grapsed his shoulders while her body rocked and swayed until the strong tide inside of her began to ebb and eventually subsided. She was left panting on the pillows. Her hands cradled his head. She let go and he dried his face on the sheets and then gently kissed her thighs and stomach. Then he was on top. She began to feel his rhythm again, and he moved more assertively and then they rocked harder and harder until a gentle purring sound seemed to rise from deep within him, first only in his chest and then more loudly, until he let out a long moan.

*   *   *

Several days later Mrs. Shangkuan boarded her return flight at Pudong Airport. In her purse, next to her navy-blue American passport and pale-green Chinese identity card, she carried several embossed envelopes with two sets of photographs of her son and new daughter-in-law folded in fine tissue paper. In the first set, against the backdrop of a traditional Shanghai lane house and another with the skyline of the Bund reflected in the dark river, Kevin wore the charcoal pin-striped suit she had ordered for him at the fabric market for a pittance, and a very expensive-looking tie that the tailor had thrown in when she had ordered a jacket to be done overnight. Lin Yi wore red. There were several other portraits of the young couple at Yuyuan Gardens with Kevin in the same outfit but Lin Yi in American bridal white. All of them were traditional wedding images, produced for the purpose of assuaging the anger of her in-laws over this shotgun wedding, and of creating the impression that all was well in the Shangkuan clan.

Mrs. Shangkuan put the photographs back in

her purse. She fingered a small jade horse that hung around her neck on a piece of red string, which Dr. Wang had given her. The plane took off, gaining rapidly in height, and tilted toward the East. The rice paddies of Pudong suddenly dropped away beneath the plane and the China Sea swung into view, with the sky above a velvety deep red from the quickly setting sun. She gently rubbed the jade horse between her fingers, cried, and laughed through her tears, and then cried some more.

89

INHERITANCE

The doorbell buzzed persistently, a sharp and rattling sound over the faint din of afternoon traffic that coursed fourteen stories below. Zaiyong hesitated for a moment before opening his apartment door. Instead of a delivery guy who'd gotten off at the wrong floor he saw a man in a dark suit through the screen door, and waited. It was mid-afternoon on a Friday, and he was at home at this unusual hour because it had not been worth going to the office after his return flight from Beijing had been two hours late. "Are you Qun Lisheng's son?" the man asked, his face cut into hundreds of tiny squares by the pattern of the screen door's wire mesh.

When he heard his father's name Zaiyong instantly felt sweat forming on his scalp. For a moment he thought of just slamming the door shut. Instead he stared straight at the young man who was dressed in an ivory shirt and a badly fitted suit, typical of public servants. He was unwilling to answer the question but also felt nervous about not obeying an official's request.

"Excuse me, you are Qun Lisheng's son?" the man repeated and glanced at a paper he held in his hand. "I am from the government and have something important to discuss with you."

"What do you need?" Zaiyong said in what came out almost as a hiss, and tightened his hand around the edge of the door. He was suddenly aware that he was wearing his plastic slippers, and that the man could probably just push through the screen door with a fist if he was not quick enough.

Instead the man asked softly, "May I come in for a moment?" and glanced to the side. Zaiyong followed his eyes and caught the nosy gaze of one of his neighbors standing in her doorway, staring at them. The narrow-faced woman scrunched up her nose as if to smell what was going on. It was rare than anyone got past the uniformed doormen and came up unannounced. Was he in trouble? Zaiyong worried, and opened the screen door. His building was one of six identical towers set amidst a landscaped area crisscrossed by narrow walkways lined with pruned shrubs, gazebos for bike storage, and squat tiled buildings made to look like shiny pagodas meant for garbage sorting, but used as workshops by traveling craftsmen to fix household appliances, shoes, and bikes. Almost nobody passed through the etched glass doors without having called up first. His neighbor kept staring and Zaiyong wanted to get this meeting over with out of her view.

"It's not convenient," Zaiyong said with a dry throat.

"It will only take a minute," the man said in what sounded like an apology. "I need you to look at some papers."

Wordlessly Zaiyong stepped to the side and let the man enter. He does not look threatening, Zaiyong thought, and gestured toward the living room in resignation. A small glass table and a narrow black shelving unit were pushed against the wall in the room dominated by a hulking tan leather couch like a cow separated from its herd. Zaiyong remained in the doorway, effectively forcing the man to either stand in the middle of the room or, as he did now, take a seat.

"This is about your late father, Qun Lisheng," the man said and took a paper folder from a scuffed briefcase.

"I have no concerns with my late father's business," Zaiyong said. Quickly he squeezed his lips to keep down the surge of anger and hurt that welled up suddenly. It rose from his stomach and tightened the insides of his mouth, anger and sorrow and then bitter shame that he did not wish to taste again. If he opened his mouth now it would spill from his lips and flood the room as a sobbing wail. It would drench the stupid couch and this pale and timid guy from the government sitting on it, drench him with the anger and hurt that Zaiyong thought he had put away in the years since his father's death four years ago. He was furious that this anger could still get the better of him, and swallowed hard to get rid of the acrid taste.

"Zaiyong, your father would not want you here," Uncle had said on the phone when Zaiyong had learned of Father's death. The memory of Uncle's voice on the phone forced Zaiyong to blink back tears. The realization that he was about to cry made him even angrier, and he felt the same cold sweat on his forearms and temples that he had felt back then, when Uncle had announced, "You have caused enough sadness for this family." The sentence had hit him like a slap across the face.

At first Zaiyong had been too stunned to respond. "What?" he had blurted out finally, shocked and at a loss for a reply. When he had realized that Uncle had already hung up he had snapped his phone shut and walked out of the studio where he was working that day. "Zaiyong?" his assistant, an over-eager American-born Chinese kid on a study abroad program in Shanghai, had called out after him. "Is everything okay, Zaiyong?" but he had not turned around.

Nothing had been okay after that for a long while. The following week, when he should have been settling his family's affairs in his hometown after Father's death, Zaiyong had stayed holed up in his apartment. Who had sat to the right of Father's coffin during the three-day wake? It must have been Uncle's good-for-nothing son, Zaiyong's little asshole cousin, who greeted the guests in Zaiyong's place, handed out the family's gifts for the mourners, and paid the monk and the undertaker.

Zaiyong had stayed shut in his apartment for days, unable to face anybody who had heard about Father's death and would be prone to console him. Then he went back to work. He threw himself into projects for the following winter, and over four difficult years of working tirelessly he succeeded in putting much of the pain out of his head. He'd finished projects during the Autumn and New Year's holidays while his co-workers visited their families, and when he got another promotion he finally bought his apartment on Pan Yu Lu. He remembered the day he signed the papers, giddy with excitement in the agent's bland office, but there had been nobody to celebrate with him. Since then he'd worked hard to assemble a group of friends, and he'd started to think of the apartment as his home.

"I work with the provincial government's chamber of worker's rights." The man interrupted Zaiyong's thoughts and looked up expectantly. Zaiyong swallowed hard and stared at him. What the hell did he want? What was this guy doing here sitting on his couch, in this apartment that Zaiyong had made into his home without anybody's help? And now this jerk thought that he could just ring the doorbell, mention Father's name, and simply because he worked for the government, tear open my heart?

"I have no concern with my late father's affairs," Zaiyong repeated with all of the formality he could muster. It felt good to spit out this angry sentence, and Zaiyong continued in the same tone to keep his emotions at bay, and make it sound as if this were merely a business matter.

"I request you to leave my apartment now," he ordered the man and felt a hint of relief when he saw a flicker of worry on the man's face. The man looked away quickly, perhaps fearing that direct eye contact could provoke Zaiyong to strike at him. Zaiyong crossed his arms but allowed his anger to push down the sadness that had so unexpectedly surged up.

"There was an investigation," the government official meekly continued. He raised his eyes to address Zaiyong but kept his head down, as if still not entirely sure whether Zaiyong wouldn't lunge.

"Your father did not die in an accident," he added more confidently. "The plant manager had been getting kickbacks from local collectives, and your father had found out about it. When they poured the grain into the silo that your father was cleaning, it was done on purpose…" The man's voice trailed off, hesitant about how to describe the manner in which Zaiyong's father had died. *Foreman buried alive in grain silo accident*, Zaiyong had read in the local paper that a schoolmate had mailed to him a few weeks afterwards. *Workers struggle for two days to empty silo and locate buried body.*

During the final summer just before Zaiyong had moved to Beijing on a scholarship, when he and his father had still been close, he had worked for the shipping company with the hulking silos near the river where his father was employed. The early shifts started as soon as one of the long flat container barges had docked alongside the low wall of the dirty canal. For several weeks that humid summer when the morning sky was streaked with yellow and gray bands of clouds, Zaiyong would jump on top of the grain dunes that filled the ship even before the barge had been properly tied up. With both hands he grabbed a huge metal vacuum tube that hung from a loading crane above him like the intestines of a large, half-slaughtered beast. Then the vacuum was switched on, and with the tube suddenly alive with jerky, spasmic movements he began to suck the grain out of the barge and into the bellies of the vast silos that lined the canal. It took an entire day to stand alone in the grain dunes in a boat and suck up the wheat. Zaiyong was careful not to move the heavy pipe too quickly or let go lest it swing and knock him out with its crazy, whipping motions. Soon the dunes started shifting under his feet, and from that point until the last grain had been siphoned out he had to keep climbing up the steadily downward sliding wheat to keep from falling. Finally the vacuum pipe would scrape along the barge's metal bottom, and at the end of the day the boat would be empty. Using a yellow plastic remote control dangling from the crane above, Zaiyong would switch off the vacuum, killing its snaps and jerks, and then move it up and out of the way where its hungry mouth would dangle from under the crane's long spindly legs until the next ship pulled in. He would then climb out of the barge on a rusty ladder that had been covered by grain at the beginning of the shift. He remembered an evening when the barge's captain and the silo workers got into a fight because it had taken past the end of the shift to empty the boat. The two men yelled and cursed at each other furiously while Zaiyong was left to drift on the container down the canal, a few feet of slimy, brackish water separating him from land. Finally another worker took pity on the boy, and with the help of a wench, pulled the barge back to shore.

Zaiyong shivered when his body relived the sensation of standing inside a deep container atop the shifting heap of grains. How far the sky had seemed from the bottom of the ship! He had always thought it strange to be standing with his shoes on top of grain that would become food later, and how he would find grains in his hair, ears, between his toes and in his crotch even after he had dumped what seemed like kilos of wheat from shoes and pockets and washed up after his shift. Father had been so pleased to have found Zaiyong, his only child, this well-paying job at his company where he could save up a bit of money for university. He had even taken a day off from work to take Zaiyong to the train station at summer's end, and checked twice to be sure that Zaiyong's hard-earned money was safely placed inside a special pocket Mother had sewn into his thin jacket.

"Huhmm," the man interrupted Zaiyong's thoughts to get his attention. "As I was saying, there was a formal investigation. The plant manager was found guilty of corruption, which your father had reported. He was also convicted of manslaughter. He is in prison waiting for the sentence to be carried out." The man waited for a moment as if to gauge Zaiyong's reaction to this news. When no response came he continued.

"The court has awarded the family a settlement for your father's death," the man said now with the confidence of someone sharing good news.

"I don't want the money," Zaiyong retorted sharply. "I don't want any settlement, and I would like you to leave."

Again he tapped into the anger he had felt earlier. It felt good to let it out.

"Please leave now! I have no business with you, and I do not wish to receive any of your money!" His voice was full and strong now, like the voice of the men in the shipyard many summers ago who had to be heard over the roar of huge machines.

"Mr. Qun, it is *your* money," the man said plaintively. "It has taken quite a while to research your address, and as you know, you're the only direct relative."

Zaiyong moved a step into the room to clear the doorway. He was hot after having just felt a shiver, and urgently wanted the man to leave.

"I have an official money order in the amount of 466,400 yuan in your name." The official held up a piece of paper with several seals. "As your parents' only child you are the closest living relative."

Zaiyong reflexively raised his shoulders, as if expecting a blow.

"I do not want your money," he repeated mechanically, but his voice still strong.

"It is not *my* money," the man said, almost

pleadingly. "It is *your* money. Money in your name. Because of what happened with your father . . . "

He did not finish the sentence and took a breath, as if to gain strength.

"If you refuse it the money will simply go back to the government. All you need to do is sign the check and deposit it at your bank."

"I don't want to be included in the settlement," Zaiyong said and looked away. "Father and I did not get along well and I've made my life here without his help."

He stopped. He was ashamed to have talked like this to a stranger and stunned how acutely he still felt the loss. He did not want those feelings to come back and took a deep breath.

"I want you to leave," he repeated loudly, almost shouting now. "I told you I have no business with Father's affairs. That was his decision four years ago, and I've managed on my own ever since."

He stepped into the hallway and opened the front door. The man scrambled to his feet.

"May I leave this paperwork with you?"

When he heard the man's timid voice Zaiyong felt embarrassed at having shouted. It's not this guy's fault, he thought. He's just delivering a letter from the government. But it's also not my fault that there was a corrupt official! And I certainly don't want money that will make me think about Mom and Dad every day!

"Yes. No. It doesn't matter," he said in response to the man's request and stared at the floor. The man placed a folder on the small table in the hallway.

"Mr. Qun," he then said apologetically, "I am very sorry to bring this terrible news about your father's death. This must be very difficult."

Difficult it had surely been, when he hadn't been allowed to attend Father's funeral. But how could this news, delivered by this guy who had landed on his doorstep like a swallow in winter, change that now? The money wasn't going to restore his family, Zaiyong thought, with his parents gone. Worse, Uncle would think him greedy if he accepted the money. "You bring shame to this family," Zaiyong could almost hear Uncle's nasty hiss, "but you'll take your dead Father's money!" The thought made him furious. He stared at the floor and noticed the man's scuffed suede shoes. The sight made him think of a pair of suede shoes he'd bought in his hometown with Father before University that he'd worn for years after he first moved to Beijing.

The official said, "I am sorry to bring you this news. And I've left the papers on your table."

The door closed and Zaiyong's shoulders and arms suddenly ached, as if he had been doing reps with the chipped, cast-iron dumbbells he kept on the floor near the couch. He slouched to the bedroom and dropped on the bed. He turned his face toward the window so as not to look at the pale green paint he had so carefully chosen for the walls. The color now seemed to smart his eyes, and the framed black-and-white photographs of European cities that he had bought with his friend Claudia in a gallery in Beijing suddenly seemed pretentious and even ugly to him.

He stared at the ceiling. Father had been murdered by a corrupt official? And they were going to give him 500,000 yuan to make up for it? When Father had told him not to visit his hometown again, he'd been stunned. But if that was the way it was going to be, he'd decided back then, then he wasn't going to ask for anything of them! The thoughts jumbled in his head, and for a moment he didn't know whether the money was something Father had left him, or came from somewhere else. Even when he'd heard, a while after Father's death, that Uncle had sold the family's apartment at a tidy profit he hadn't asked for a single fen. Not a fen of his rightful inheritance.

Zaiyong got up and searched for his cigarettes. He lit one and stood by the window, trying not to let the anger get the better of him. What did any of this matter now, years after Father had told him during his last visit to his hometown shortly before Mother's death, that it would be better if their only son stayed away, given the way he chose to live his life. Chose to live his life! As if anyone would choose to go through all of this darkness alone. Oh yes, he had managed to start life for himself, but he couldn't call it a choice. As if he would have chosen to make Mother so unhappy, during her final months when she seemed to be drowning in the soft-cushioned chair, constantly shivering under the quilt and yet her face shiny with a thin film of sweat. The women who tended to her had asked increasingly pointed questions about his lack of a fiancée, and finally they had appeared to Zaiyong like a circle of sharp-eyed crows hopping around a defenseless baby rabbit.

"Chose to live his life."

The sentence rattled in Zaiyong's head, clanging against other memories that had become unmoored by the unexpected visitor.

"Chose to live his life."

As if anyone would choose to go through this

frightening emptiness. As if he had chosen to become the studious loner who preferred books to a social life, and who had watched his classmates start dating girls one-by-one while he felt that light and air were being sucked from the world. He could have joined so easily the ranks of students who left the first-year camaraderie of crowded dorm rooms with their smelly bunks and towel fights for the happiness of a couple, with the attendant benefits of a residence permit for an apartment, the combined income that could pay for it, and the cessation of everyone's prying queries. He could so easily have clasped one of the girls' hands to pull him from the brink of loneliness and despair yawning before him.

Oh, a choice! He remembered taking a bus with a beautiful girl to the Summer Palace. He had stood next to the girl looking over the lake choked with huge, wavy-edged blue-green lotus leaves without finding the courage to touch her arm, or brush back her hair and lean in for a kiss. Another girl had been delighted to accept an invitation for a simple dinner the week before, wearing a nice blouse and make-up that made her eyes stand out brightly. Then they had gone to a screening at the university's film society and the girls' hand dropped, as if accidentally, on his thigh. He had sat there absolutely frozen until the girl retracted her hand, and later he caught a strange look in her eyes, which alternately blamed him but also signaled her shame that the problem rested with herself.

He had seen his best friend at university also blame herself for another awkward afternoon at the Summer Palace when the two of them had failed to kiss. The sun had hung low over the park in a hazy sky, and the lotus leaves swayed lightly above the water that couldn't be seen but gave off a sickly sweet smell. There were couples dotting the stone banister along the quiet shore, and Zaiyong had known perfectly well what had been expected of him. Easy. So easy it would have been to lean over and kiss her. And then he had felt terrible when he saw that his friend nervously adjusted her hair and sweater and brushed her hand over her mouth when she thought he was not looking, thinking that there was surely something wrong with her. He'd thought himself cursed for pulling this wonderful woman who so much wanted love into the darkness that was his alone. He had tried to be a good son but ultimately could not drown her heart just so that he could live above the surface.

"My studies keep me busy," was Zaiyong's standard response to his parents' weekly phone call during those years at university.

"We are so proud of you," they responded, both of them on the line. "With your degree you'll be able to provide for a happy family."

Zaiyong pressed the dirty plastic receiver to his ear to hear over the din of the hallway where the dorm's only phone was located.

"I miss you," he said instead of responding and quickly hung up, breathing a sigh of relief to have gotten through a call before Mother could pose her customary question – whether or not he had met any girls.

He had saved money and resolved to overcome his shyness in the massage parlors around the bus terminal in Beijing. On rickety tables covered with vinyl sheets he lay rigid and sweating, his anxiety defeating the girl's efforts to have him relax so that she could slide her hand inside his worn-out underwear. Some of the massage girls, confused by the lack of a response, had warmed up their hands and tried another time, or reached for a different kind of oil. But nothing worked. Finally he got off the table, quickly pulled on socks, pants and shoes, and tipped the girl who stuck the money into a small cotton purse hidden in her short apron.

"Come back soon and I won't charge you extra," they had said while looking at him with their kohl-lined eyes, "we've all got trouble sometimes." Usually with a red face, Zaiyong made it past the woman in the front and out the door into the busy streets where nobody cared whether he'd been with a girl or not.

Then sometimes late at night at university he had a hushed and hurried conversation on the same orange hallway phone from which he called his parents on Sunday afternoons. But these conversations, dialed to numbers he had found scribbled on a bathroom wall in the language building, left his throat dry with anxious anticipation. A few times he had walked past Dongdan Park in the early evening but each time he had been too scared to enter, repulsed by the scene of men passing through the bushes with their eyes full of longing and fear. Finally, he signed out with the sleepy security guard at the university's front gates and rode a lumbering bus through Beijing's silent avenues to the many-entranced long-distance bus terminal. For a few minutes he walked back and forth near a specific vendor in the underground terminal and debated with himself whether to turn around, all the while furtively peeking from under his hooded jacket at travelers stopping to buy cigarettes. People waited nearby in silence, their hands buried in their pockets and their faces turned away from the draft, and then filed out the heavy rubber-edged doors to catch their bus to Chengde, Harbin, or as far as Kunming. Zaiyong stood near the vendor, eager to embark on a closer but far more precarious journey. After a word or two, and a glance with a stranger held just a moment, and then another moment, and in any case longer than expected, he followed a man to a cheap hotel nearby or, after checking all sides, into the service area behind the public latrines.

And there, while he struggled not to retch from the rank smell of the latrine and the naked fear of being discovered by the guard, Zaiyong felt as if he found himself for moments at a time. When the other man touched him the shame and the repulsion of his own body that made him want *this*, this hated and craved moment when another man held him, slipped away ever so briefly. The shame dropped away and Zaiyong felt light as he had finally reached the surface after having been pushed under water for too long, and he tasted a freedom that he could find only inside of himself and nowhere else.

For a few weeks after each of these encounters Zaiyong's mind won out over his body. He would convince himself that this had been his last trip to the terminal. But slowly the fear of getting arrested and the shame of wanting to hold another man were eclipsed by a stronger dread. His fellow students were exactly like him, quick-witted boys and girls from the provinces who through hard work had earned a coveted spot in the top tier of the national high school exams. But their good-natured invitations to join a party or a meal sounded like locks snapping shut all around him, leaving Zaiyong alone and sinking into airless isolation. He spent days in the unheated library, devoured hot noodles by himself in the crowded cafeteria, and lay awake in his bunk trying to draw a full breath but feeling his lungs getting more and more constricted. He listened to the deep and even breathing of the seven young men in the bunk beds in his room. A panic seized him that while they dreamt vividly of life after graduation he would suffocate that night.

"Zaiyong doesn't like girls," one of the other boys had declared sharply when he declined to join them on their way to crashing the women's college's social hours one day.

"Leave him alone," another guy defended him, "he hangs out with Raisa all the time, and you know she's picky about the guys she lets near her!"

"I'm telling you, he's not into pussy," the other guy said and stared at Zaiyong. Zaiyong willed himself not to blink or look away but he also did not respond. He had the courage to sneak off campus to meet men whose names he never learned and risk arrest, public humiliation, and expulsion from university. He'd heard about the electroshock therapy to cure people like him, and even jail time for unrepentants.

But it would have taken more courage than venturing out on his clandestine excursions, courage Zaiyong did not have back then, to set the other guy straight in front of everyone, once and for all: "Yes, I'm not screwing Raisa, so leave me the fuck alone."

It had taken enormous courage to enter the grimy massage parlors near the bus terminal, and it had taken courage to call from the dorm phone for fear that a government trap had been set up on this line. But finally the greatest challenge had been to visit his hometown and face his aunties' questions. Soon after his arrival Zaiyong sat amidst a group of women in boldly patterned blouses wielding cigarettes, and enjoying a bit of liquor with their afternoon cup of tea. A few of these women were directly related to Zaiyong, but all of them were considered aunties after having fed and minded and washed him when he had toddled around in bare-bottomed pants as a little boy.

They sat around the kitchen table, Zaiyong in their midst as their favorite nephew returning from Shanghai, while his mother rested nearby with her legs wrapped in a blanket. It was a constant coming and going, with someone getting up to fetch some special honey from her house or rolling down the waistband of her new black pants to show how cleverly the rubber band had been sown in.

"Such a handsome boy and no girlfriend," they had teased him and laughed while his mother looked out the window. There was only the next building's wall but she stared as intently at it as if she were following a bird soar in the sky. "Even in Shanghai they can recognize a handsome face like our Zaiyong's," the aunties continued laughingly, a few of them winking and all of their shiny faces beaming with pride.

"Look at Zaiyong's fine shirts, and these good shoes," an auntie said, making a clucking sound, "there is no way a woman did not pick these out for him!" They all laughed and someone put more food on his plate.

"Maybe your girlfriend is too fancy to visit our

small town," another one said but the option was roundly dismissed.

"Of course even city girl knows that a future daughter-in-law must honor her parents!" someone cried out and pursed her lips as if posing for a fashion shoot.

"You can have a big-shot wedding banquet in Shanghai after you come home to visit us," they reassured him. "But your wife will realize that we can cook better than all the big-time chefs in Shanghai!" his mother's sister laughed and pinched Zaiyong as if he were a little boy.

"Your mother wants to rock a grandson!" his aunt said, now more urgently, and the sudden change in tone quieted them down.

"And Father wants to see another tiger being born," Mother added quietly, referring to the fact that both Zaiyong and his father had been born in that auspicious year.

The neighbors left. Zaiyong and his auntie sat at the table, with his mother in her low comfortable chair next to them. The kitchen suddenly felt small even though at least a dozen people had just been there. It was quiet after the noisy dinner except for his mother's labored breathing. The pots and dishes that had been brought by the gaggle of neighbors now looked mismatched and chipped. I could have sent them new dishes, Zaiyong thought and regretted not bringing more gifts from Shanghai.

Auntie sighed. "Zaiyong's not going to get married," she announced definitively, as if he were not sitting right next to her. She lit a cigarette. "My favorite nephew is not going to be a husband, or a father."

Zaiyong glanced at Mother's face, frail under wisps of hair that had once encircled her healthy cheeks. It took courage for him to remain silent and not protest this assessment, which now hung in the room like a courtroom's verdict. He looked away from Mother, and knew that she so very badly wanted him to say something and correct her sister. But he remained silent, and by saying nothing at this moment he said enough. He could not bring himself to invent another story about a girlfriend who was too busy to visit because of a demanding schedule in Shanghai.

"My only child," Mother said as if begging him to respond. Zaiyong stared at the table. When he allowed the seconds to stretch into a full minute of silence Auntie's sentence was proven true. A sound made Zaiyong look up and he caught a glance of Father standing in the doorway to the hall. Zaiyong's throat contracted, but he remained silent. Father looked at him, and then abruptly left the room. Auntie stubbed out the cigarette she had just lit and poured herself more tea.

"Who is going to cook for you?" Mother asked, a tear making its way down her cheek. "Who is going to take care of you?" she said.

Zaiyong wiped his eyes, struggling hard not to sob. He swallowed and responded, "Mom, I have an *ayi* who cooks and cleans for me, and I can take care of myself."

Auntie put a bun on the plate before him, pushing aside the food he had not touched.

"A man needs a woman to look after him!" Mother said and turned to him.

"Let's get some rest now," Auntie cut off the

conversation and rose. "Zaiyong is a good boy and will visit us again soon."

With that she adjusted the blanket around her sister's legs and fluffed the pillow behind her head.

For the next few days during the afternoons Zaiyong sat beside Mother, who was wrapped in a blanket and blue shawl, in front of their apartment building. They ate crowded dinners with neighbors, friends and family. Nights he slept on the narrow cot in Father's room, so as not to disturb Mother's badly needed rest. Zaiyong made every effort to make Mother enjoy his visit. He bought expensive tea and small soft biscuits. But on the last night she sat up in her chair and with a burst of unexpected urgency pleaded, "Visit just one time with a fiancée! So the people won't say I'm the only woman in town who will die without a grandchild!"

She sank back into her pillow, her red-rimmed eyes wet with tears. "I'll be okay," Zaiyong reassured her but realized that it was not his well-being that was at stake. He grasped her hand.

"I'm going to be fine, Mommy," he said while Father and Auntie looked at him in silence. But he was not quite sure whether he would be okay. He went outside and walked in the evening's heat, not wanting to worry his parents anymore. His skin felt cold in spite of the humidity, and he walked for hours before returning home. The next morning, when he had to leave, he gently placed his hand on Mother's forehead so as not to wake her.

"You see how much stress this is causing your mother," Father said when they reached the train station. Zaiyong saw that Father's face was animated by the dread of being alone, a dread he knew all too well from his years in Beijing and now Shanghai. Father turned away and spoke the next sentence in the direction of two uniformed guards by the turnstiles in front of the platforms.

"She is suffering enough already with the illness, so it's best if you don't visit again unless you bring a fiancée," he said quietly.

The sentence hung in the heavy, diesel-scented air between them, stilling for a moment the throngs of commuters pressing through the turnstiles and the peddlers hawking packed lunches, egg pancakes, and water. Father knew that there was no girlfriend, and that there would never be one. Zaiyong stood in the station in shock, clutching the smooth leather bag his friend Claudia had brought him as a gift from a company trip to Bangkok.

"But I was going to visit in eight weeks," Zaiyong responded. "My assistants can cover for me, and there are a few things I want to get you and Mom from Shanghai."

"Your visits are too upsetting for Mother," Father said and stared off into space. "You know how much she wants to have a grandchild."

Zaiyong hugged Father, expecting him to retract what he'd just said. But Father remained silent. Zaiyong boarded the train and fought his way into a compartment. He pushed his bag on to the rack and squeezed into a seat. When he looked out the window he could see Father on the platform. He felt his heart beating in his throat when he looked at the man who had always loved him as if he were still the boy who he could carry on his shoulders through a crowd. A couple brushed by and Father took an awkward step forward not to lose his balance. Zaiyong jumped up, jostled through the people getting onto the train and alighted on the platform. He went over to Father and, without so much as having planned to do so, kissed him on the cheeks. "Take good care, dad," Zaiyong said. "Tell Mom I love her."

Father did not respond. A sharp whistle announced the train's imminent departure and Zaiyong quickly climbed aboard just before the doors fell shut. The train started moving and Zaiyong sat down, his face buried in his bunched-up jacket. He did not know how he could persuade Father to let him visit again, and at the beginning of his long journey back to Shanghai he turned his face toward the window and permitted himself to cry silently the tears he had not wanted his parents to see.

When Zaiyong arrived for Mother's funeral several months later, the accusation that he had worsened her condition hung in the house like the heavy fabric that covered up the mirrors and windowpanes. It was August, and the stifling apartment was so crowded with mourners that for the first night Zaiyong slept fitfully sitting on a chair. Every so often he awoke with the strong sensation of his mother gently shaking him to wake up as if he were a little boy again. Zaiyong's body ached with the memory of Mother's soft palm when she held his hand on their way to school.

When he woke up in the morning he was sweaty and his back ached. The room was still filled with aunties, uncles, cousins, and neighbors. Father sat across from him staring straight ahead at the coffin. Father's eyes were open but expressionless, as if he were guarding his dead wife while asleep.

The next day, Mother's coffin was taken through town in a hearse pulled by Uncle's car. Zaiyong and Father had thrown dirt on the coffin under a sky the color of boiled cabbage. When the small group made its way back from the dusty cemetery the sky seemed to peel away its layers of haze to reveal a dark and threatening gray, and by the time they reached the apartment a terrible hail beat down on them. They rushed inside but Father could not be found anywhere. The guests waited while Zaiyong ran through the storm to check with neighbors and relatives in town. Finally the meal had to commence without the widower as the proper host. Without a word between them Zaiyong, drenched from the storm, welcomed the guests with Uncle. Father showed up long after Zaiyong's aunties had cleaned up the kitchen, packed away the food, and Zaiyong and Uncle had stiffly bid the guests farewell.

"I have to sleep," was all Father said before he stretched out on the cot without taking off his clothes.

"Do you want tea?" Zaiyong asked but Father did not respond.

"I can fix you something to eat," he added.

"It's not a man's job to heat the food," Father said curtly and lay down on his cot. "Your aunties have prepared enough food and will take care of me."

The remark stung. Zaiyong had made tea for his parents as long as he could remember. He emptied the kettle, suddenly self-conscious that he was performing woman's work. He lay down on the other cot and after hours of tossing he finally fell asleep until dawn, when the sun pried in sleek columns past the fabric covering the windows.

The two men brushed their teeth over the kitchen

sink side by side. Father struggled with the electric kettle, and Zaiyong wordlessly assumed the task of preparing breakfast for them. He needs me, he thought while setting the few dishes on the table, and he felt utterly helpless at seeing Father so bereft and withdrawn.

How could he help Father? And who would help *him*? The kitchen looked like that of a city migrant worker, with dirty dishes and garbage heaped randomly, as if nothing but Mother's touch had kept things together until now when even, toward the end, she had been too frail to get up. What am I going to do? he thought, but Father's hollowed face and withdrawn eyes kept him from thinking more about himself.

"Are you going to be okay?" Zaiyong finally asked when it was time to leave. He had left the dishes in the plastic bucket instead of quickly rinsing them.

"Your auntie is going to look after me," Father offered in response. They embraced briefly, after which Father turned and sat in a chair by the window. Zaiyong walked alone to the train station, his stomach coiled into a knot.

When Zaiyong phoned a few days after his return to Shanghai, Father's tired voice sounded far more distant than the thousand kilometers or so that actually separated them.

"I'm getting by," Father said quietly. "Just getting by."

There was silence on the line.

"Dad? Are you still there?" Zaiyong asked anxiously. "Dad?" He stared out of the window of his apartment, watching a black cat locked in one of the tiny glass-enclosed balconies on a very high floor of the building across the courtyard. The cat paced back and forth and looked longingly at the thin metal railing. Without Mother on the phone, as there had been for years until now, there was no response.

"Dad?"

"I'm here," Zaiyong heard Father say. The voice sounded even further away. Without the friendly chatter of the woman who had loved them so much and who had usually initiated and sustained their calls, a simple conversation had suddenly become impossible.

"Dad?" Zaiyong repeated and turned away from the window.

"I'm getting by," Father repeated but to Zaiyong it sounded as if the opposite were true, and that Father thought this were somehow his fault.

"Zaiyong, I can't talk to you," Father said. There was a click when Father hung up. Not "I can't talk to you *now*, I'm busy and I will call later" but "I can't talk to you." Zaiyong felt as if he had been hit in the stomach. It felt exactly the way when he had been hit once, the only time in his life, on the way home from school when another boy had challenged him to race and he had refused. Out of nowhere incredible pain in his stomach, and then as he stood doubled over the sound of other children laughing, mocking him, and then running on.

Father had hung up suddenly, as if talking to his only son were somehow dangerous, or requiring of him a strength he could not muster during this period of grief.

Letters had followed, mailed every few weeks by Zaiyong from the mailbox in the lobby at work to Father's address, but never a response. Phone calls lasted only a minute and merely confirmed that Father was alive.

"Your father does not want to speak with you!" Little Cousin had snarled when Zaiyong had finally gotten through to someone in his hometown. "He's fine but does not want to talk."

"He is my father," Zaiyong had shouted into the phone, "he is my father, you jerk!" but Little Cousin had hung up. The darkness that had surrounded him during the first years at university in Beijing had seemed impenetrable. But Father's refusal to speak had taught him that there was a deeper darkness yet, as if near the end of a black alley the ground had suddenly given way to plunge him into a bottomless well.

A few months later, while Zaiyong was rearranging images on a brightly colored screen in his advertising agency, Cousin called.

"Zaiyong, there's been an accident," he declared without any time to say hello. "Your father was killed at work." Then Uncle's voice came on the line. "We've sent you a copy of the workplace report," he said.

"What happened?" Zaiyong asked, stunned by the news. "What did he do?"

"I've sent you the papers to your work address," Uncle said. "The funeral was last week."

"There was a funeral?" Zaiyong said, incredulous. "A funeral last week?"

"Your father did not want to have contact with you. So we decided it was better for us to arrange everything ourselves."

"Uncle, what happened?" Zaiyong asked, failing to understand what he had just been told.

"You've caused enough sadness for this family,"

Uncle said. "Your father was a tiger of a man," he continued, "but with you…"

He left the sentence unfinished. Zaiyong couldn't breathe, he was so shocked. He had stood up when Cousin's voice had been on the phone but now he sat down heavily. *A tiger will never give birth to a dog*; he completed Uncle's line in his head. Father was a tiger but I'm a dog. Uncle's voice interrupted his thoughts.

"Your mother's death and now your life weighed your father down. You caused them so much sadness."

Zaiyong struggled to speak. "Uncle," he squeezed out finally. "Uncle," but he realized that Uncle had already hung up. Zaiyong sat there, stunned by the news. He tried dialing Uncle's and then Cousin's numbers but got no response, and then, also to no avail, Father's phone at home.

This had been four years ago. And for many months while sorrow circled around his head, like small pesky birds, Zaiyong had made every conceivable effort not to let them roost. For a good two years he never spent an evening alone, choosing instead to go out first to dinner and then to end up in one of two bars near his house until he was drowsy enough to go home and sleep.

And now this guy from the government with his payment of 500,000 yuan had brought all of it back. Zaiyong lay on his bed, lit another cigarette, and tried to push his father's death out of his mind again. That whole autumn after Uncle's phone was a blur in his mind. There had been weeks of summery weather that had run into fall without peaks or valleys, the way the skyline of buildings outside of Zaiyong's windows blended into a formless gray mass when the rain misted up the insides of his poorly insulated windows. There must have been a Harvest Moon Festival and a Fall Holiday but he could not recall how he had spent those days. He knew that he had art-directed two commercials right after his father's death since those videos still cycled through the city on the screens in the back of Shanghai's taxicabs. These clips had earned him the promotion to his current job. But he could not remember pitching the concept, nor auditioning the actors, nor filming in the renovated exhibition space that had been built originally in 1930 as Asia's largest slaughterhouse. He knew that he had spent weeks editing the footage and the music until the girls looked sexy and the guys looked hot, but he couldn't remember doing that. He remembered staring out of the window at a set of newly planted pine trees. And he recalled nights where he had fallen asleep, on the floor next to the couch in the living room, after taking a tablet that made him feel as if he could see his own thoughts through a thick pane of glass.

"Fuck!" Zaiyong yelled and pounded his fist on the expensive comforter on his mattress. "Fuck!" he yelled again but could not cry.

* * *

A few days after the government official's visit to his home, Zaiyong met a friend for dinner at an outdoor Thai restaurant in the French Concession. "I don't need the money," he explained to her while she set her shopping bags on another chair next to the koi pond that surrounded the dark wooden deck, and tied her hair into a loose ponytail. "My father did not accept me as part of the family, and I made peace with that."

"Let's order first," his friend said gently.

When the food arrived he picked a tiny pink shrimp from a glazed black plate, and nodded when the waiter asked whether he wanted more beer.

"I have my apartment, I have my job. He did not want to be my father any longer, so why should some provincial court decide now that I have to be his son? What right do they have? Not now, just because this idiot found out where I lived."

"What did the government guy say you had to do to get the money?" Zaiyong's friend asked, finally ready to focus.

"I said I didn't want it!" Zaiyong said forcefully. "The guy thought I felt bad that my father died not in an accident. But what do I care now! My father wanted me to build my own life without his help, and I did exactly that!"

"I'm sorry, Zaiyong," she said and put her hand on his arm. "The guy is just doing his job. I still think you should think about this a bit." She paused for a moment.

"I'm sorry to say this, but what happened between you and your father is maybe no longer so important," she ventured. "Look how much your life has changed from that time four years ago! Are you still angry at your uncle?"

"He sold my parents' house and I didn't take a single fen!" Zaiyong said loudly.

"So you've already made your point. If you don't take this settlement the money will just go to the government. You could give it to somebody else!"

"I'm not making a point," he said. "I don't want

their money. Accepting it would mean that I forgive him."

She smiled at him. "This is no longer about your father, sweetie. This is about the government for once doing something right. All it takes is for you to take the papers to the bank."

After dinner Zaiyong found his friend a taxi. When she had left he stood at the curb and for a minute or so looked at the large, white moon that floated directly above the quiet intersection before him. He waved on another taxi and instead walked, with his hands buried in the pockets of his short cotton jacket. He did not take the direct route to his home but passed through quiet streets until he reached the plain-looking door of a bar next to a convenience store. Inside he settled in the corner at a tall metal table that was cool to the touch, and ordered a whisky. The throbbing music enveloped him like steam in a sauna, and the whisky pleasantly tickled his throat. For a few moments he traced the "*IKEA*" stamped on the bottom of the glass with a thin black straw.

Then he glanced up, casually, just to take in who was here. The room was about half full, not bad for a weekday. But it wasn't as if Zaiyong was looking for anything. It was just nice to sit there, soothed by the knowledge that if he was interested in anyone that person would at least be open to chatting, even if ultimately they decided there wasn't much of a connection. He felt no pressure. He was just going to drink this one whiskey, walk home, and then go to sleep with the buzz that was just now descending on his mind. And that would let him forget about the whole business with Father's money.

"Another whisky," a waiter interrupted him and set another glass next to Zaiyong's half-full drink on the table.

"I didn't order another one," Zaiyong protested.

"It's from this gentleman sitting right over there," the waiter said and pointed vaguely toward the bar's front.

Zaiyong saw a man who held up a glass, or maybe he was just putting it down. Had he raised the glass to him? Kind of cute, Zaiyong decided, although he couldn't see much of the man's face in the bar's dim light. He can buy me a drink but *I'm* gonna make the first move, Zaiyong thought. He gulped down his first whisky and picked up the fresh drink. He walked over and sat down next to the guy.

"Thanks for the drink," he said and then stared straight ahead. Still cute, Zaiyong thought after another glance but then his courage was spent.

For a few moments both of them stared straight ahead, across the bar. When the next song was over Zaiyong asked, "Are you from Shanghai?"

He had turned his head only slightly to ask the question when something in the man's face caught his attention. He quickly swiveled his body a bit to get a better look, angling to see him in the little light provided by a metal lamp attached to the bar.

"Hey, don't I know you?" he added and scrutinized the other man's face. God, have I met him in here? Zaiyong thought, and then blood rushed to his face in embarrassment. Have I slept with him?

"Oh, heavens," the man stuttered. "Heavens, yes, hmmm, we met a few days ago," he stuttered. "But just now, a minute ago, I didn't realize that this was you sitting over there . . ." and he gestured toward the table where he had sent Zaiyong the drink.

"Hold on! You're the government official!" Zaiyong said incredulously. "You're the government official who came to my house the other day. You're the guy who wanted to give me 500,000 yuan."

"I didn't realize that was you over there," the man said, pointing again at the far corner of the bar as if Zaiyong were still sitting there and not next to him. "I just saw you . . ."

Zaiyong took a long sip from his drink. "This is very weird," he said. "Well, I wouldn't have guessed that you would come to this kind of bar."

He remembered the man to be smaller from the visit to his apartment several days before, but now he seemed to be close to his own height. He remembered the dark blue suit and yellowish, polyester shirt and casually glanced at the man's outfit. Tonight he had put on faded denim, a shirt with a Ferrari logo on the short sleeves, but the same scuffed shoes he'd worn a few days before. Again Zaiyong was reminded of his own shoes during his student days in Beijing. He's definitely not from Shanghai, Zaiyong thought, and tonight is clearly his big night out.

"This is my first time in this place," the other man said, sounding apologetic. "In my hometown there are no bars like this, and when I'm here in Shanghai I usually stay in a hotel with my colleagues so I cannot go out by myself. I also have a cousin here but didn't tell her this time that I'm here for work. Otherwise I'd have to be at her house every night and eat with her family. They don't know about me, and there's no way my parents can find out." He took a large sip of whisky but grimaced at the taste.

"And I saw you over there but didn't recognize you," he concluded.

"It's okay," Zaiyong said, sensing the need to reassure him. "And thanks for the drink," he added. "This is probably the only bar where you'd find anybody tonight," he explained. "There's another bar on Fridays, but it's very crowded and more expensive, with a dance floor. It's been closed and then reopened in different places a few times, and is kind of hard to find."

He liked to show off his knowledge of the big city. He was also flattered by the attention and moved by the guy's obvious nervousness. He signaled the waiter to bring two more drinks and they sat in silence for a bit. He's quite cute, Zaiyong thought, and enjoyed feeling the other man's eyes on him.

"So how long are you in Shanghai for?" Zaiyong asked, and shifted in his seat so his thigh came to rest against the other man's leg.

"I have to leave tomorrow night," he responded without moving his leg. "When you opened the door I thought you were so attractive," he added. He immediately fell silent again, as if he were surprised at his own bold statement.

Zaiyong laughed. "But you didn't recognize me right now when you sent over the drink! I guess I'm lucky that it was me sitting there tonight!" He had wanted to make a joke but immediately sensed the other man's worry that he had done something wrong. To reassure him he put his hand on the man's shoulder.

"It's okay," he said without removing his hand. "It's hard to see in here anyways." He saw the man's face relax.

"When I talked to you the other day, about the government check –," the man ventured, but Zaiyong interrupted him.

"I'd rather not talk about that." He felt the drink getting to his head. The guy's leg felt good and warm against his thigh.

"I gotta work early tomorrow," Zaiyong said after a while and stubbed out his cigarette. He could spot a flicker of worry in the other man's eyes. "So if you wanna come over that would be fine," he added casually and gathered his phone and wallet from the bar.

* * *

"I had been hoping the whole time that you would invite me to come with you," the man said later, while they were lying in their underwear on Zaiyong's bed.

"You shouldn't have worried," Zaiyong reassured him and lifted himself up to look into his face.

"Wasn't it obvious?" He was charmed by the guy's sincerity. "You're very handsome, and I'm happy that we met like this tonight." He was flattered by the guy's excitement. "It's just strange that I didn't realize this about you when you were here a few days ago."

The other man began to explain. "Well, it was not a happy visit for you, I'm sure. I'm sorry if I brought up sad memories . . ."

Zaiyong stopped him.

"I'd rather not talk about it," he said, although he'd raised the topic.

Then he kissed the man on the lips, briefly, before

taking both of his wrists to pin his arms over his head, not really hard but leaving no doubt that he was not going to wait for him to figure things out. He could feel the man's excitement ripple through his shoulders and chest, and said with false brightness, "Let's make this trip to Shanghai worth your while."

The guy's skin tasted of smoke, and something soapy but sharp that was the trace of cologne or bodywash he must have used earlier. His arms and legs were more solid than Zaiyong's, and he now strained against Zaiyong's grip and pressed his hips against him in a way that made Zaiyong feel like a beginner for a moment. Then they both became equals, Zaiyong's experience matched evenly by the guy's strong, affirming hunger.

* * *

A good while later Zaiyong got up and returned with a moist towel and a bottle of water. The guy woke up, saw Zaiyong, and quickly sat up.

"It's okay with me if you want to spend the night," Zaiyong said, and put his hand on the man's arm. He sat down next to him and within minutes the two men, who had looked so much like brothers when they had left the bar a bit over an hour earlier, fell asleep in each other's arms.

Zaiyong had not pulled the shades during the night and woke to an unfamiliarly bright room. He got up quickly, surprised that he had slept in the nude until past dawn. After a swift check in the kitchen and bathroom he confirmed with a glance at the front door's dangling chain lock that the guy had left.

While he dialed his work number he reached with the other hand into the shower to turn on the hot water.

"I'm gonna be late," he cheerfully said over the sound of rushing water.

"We are on location already," his American assistant replied anxiously.

"Calm down," Zaiyong said and added in English, "*chill out*, Kevin."

He hung up before his assistant could respond. That was fun last night, he thought while he toweled his hair in front of the bathroom mirror and turned on the radio. Then he stepped into the bedroom to the beat of a new pop princess tune that he had used recently as the soundtrack for a fashion event.

He picked out a white linen shirt, pale beige pants, and put on a thin leather necklace with a small metal tiger. Good fun, he thought again while riding down in the elevator to the lobby and smiled to himself. And actually really nice. He was pleased at having had such a good night in the middle of the week, and stepped briskly into the street.

In the taxi to the office Zaiyong fingered the tiger around his neck while making a few calls. The taxi moved fast, its driver determined to get across each intersection just at the moment when the light had already turned red.

* * *

"Mr. Qun Zaiyong?" a woman's voice barked on the speakerphone when Zaiyong picked up a call later that afternoon in his office. "Qun Zaiyong? You forgot your ID and bank card at our bank this morning."

"What bank?" Zaiyong asked and leaned over this desk to pick up the receiver. "What are you talking about?"

"Are you Qun Zaiyong?" the woman on the line repeated impatiently, saying his name extra-loud, as if he was a child.

He took out his wallet with one hand and looked for his bankcard. "What bank are you calling from?" he asked when he could not find the card.

"Are you or are you not Qun Zaiyong?" the woman said again.

"I am," Zaiyong said, and waited for instructions on what to do next.

Twenty minutes later Zaiyong stood at a bank counter and signed several forms.

"We need your parents' names as a security check," the teller said and looked at Zaiyong.

"Qun Lisheng, Yenbo Xui Li," he said after a short pause. When he returned the forms the teller glanced at him, then back at the papers in her hand, and then handed him his bankcard and ID.

"You're lucky someone found these and turned them in," the girl smiled at him.

Zaiyong thanked her, and then walked through the lobby. He stopped at the ATM by the door to get cash.

He had already reached the sidewalk when he glanced at the printout from the ATM. It was a sunny day, and light reflected off a stack of tall windowpanes leaning against an open storefront next to the bank. Inside the store a man was cutting a large piece of glass at a worktable surrounded by mirrors and more panes of various sizes and shapes that reflected each other and made the store look much larger than it was.

Zaiyong had stopped and now stared at the printout. He turned and re-entered the bank.

"628,290 yuan," the teller confirmed after a quick exchange and while handing back to Zaiyong his ID. "The deposit that you made this morning cleared right away since it was an official government check. But you'll have to wait till tomorrow until you can withdraw it."

Zaiyong walked out of the bank again, past the store with the windowpanes. For a brief moment, just as he passed the small space filled with its countless rectangles of reflecting glass, it looked as if there were many, many more men like Zaiyong out there. Some of them were sharply etched and clearly discernible in the afternoon light, looking as if they were moving along a brightly-lit stage, while others appeared half-hidden in the darker corners of the store, pale and partial reflections sinking into mirror after mirror like the generations passing on, from father to son and to other men beyond.

ULRICH BAER

129

THE LESSONS OF TAI CHI

At twenty minutes before seven on a Sunday morning in late May, a rumbling diesel engine startled the neighbors of a vast and dusty construction site at the intersection of Shaanxi Road and Huaihai Road from their sleep. A bulldozer took aim at a remaining row of decrepit lane houses at the edge of the construction site. Most of their façades had been torn away already, and a film of powdery yellow dust covered broken furniture, faded posters, bunched-up, dirty clothes and rotting mattresses. A woman bicycled past the construction site's fence, which was covered with poster-sized photographs of garish magenta flowers and gossamer gingko leaves.

"For heaven's sake, cover yourself up!" the woman exclaimed with a shudder when she glimpsed the torn-open houses through a gap in the fence. The sight of the broken furniture and ruined walls reminded her of the decrepit room she called home. Disgusting! You could see the innards hanging from the feeble frames as if the tenants had vacated the building just minutes ago. Her place was quite like it, with the shabby wallpaper peeling off and rust stains blooming on the walls. But they hadn't taken a bulldozer to it yet. She sublet it from a man whose motives she didn't trust but who had allowed her to fall behind on the rent. This morning she had carefully put on black leggings, a skirt, and a turtleneck. She had taken some time to put on make-up and select a few silver bangles, concentrating on completing her look in an effort to ward off awareness of this tenuous arrangement.

"What do you think it took for me to look like this today?" she hurled when she glimpsed the torn up buildings, angry at the city for revealing its intimate parts without covering up. "Why do I have to see this?" She made a huge effort every morning to look respectable and even like someone to be admired. From the age of ten there hadn't been a single day when she hadn't been perfectly put together. Now, close to her thirties, there was no chance she would let anyone realize that she was down to a single decent blouse which she carefully rinsed each evening and then dried overnight on a wire hanger. People still turned their heads in admiration when she emerged each morning, looking impeccable, from the moldy and altogether horrid place for which she owed months of rent even though it was not fit to house a dog.

But still it was a place to sleep. Her single fear was that she would either be thrown out by her landlord or that the place would be bulldozed to give way to a developer's rapacious dreams. She couldn't think of what she would do then. She had trembled when an elderly neighbor had mentioned casually, a few days before, that someone had offered him money to move out, quite a bit of money, which meant their homes were soon likely to be demolished.

"Off to teach your lessons, Ms. Huang?" That same neighbor had bowed to her this morning. "You look beautiful as always."

"Yes, no time like early morning!" She had responded, trying to sound breezy and unconcerned, and pedaled off. She hoped he had not overheard her curse this morning, once when she realized that someone had stolen the soap left in the shared bathroom and then again when the pen she used to touch up her scuffed boots had dried up. From her looks nobody could know that her income was far below that of the migrant workers' who now stood staring at her pedaling past the construction site. At least that's what she hoped. She patted her ponytail with one hand, causing the silver bangles around her wrist to jangle down her black sleeve.

"We've all got some standards to uphold," she thought and exhaled deeply to focus on what lay ahead.

A few blocks later she swung one leg over her rusty bike and glided along the sidewalk up to Fuxing Park. She locked her bike to a post and passed a vendor cooking on a portable stove in a narrow doorway. From her bag she fished a crumpled five-yuan note and made an effort to smile at the man warmly.

"Two pancakes," she said cheerfully, extending the note and relishing the fragrant steam.

A boy next to the man quickly folded two pancakes into a cellophane bag.

"Two for six," the man behind the stove said, his face as stonily immobile as the busts of Marx and Engels on their pedestal in the nearby park.

"I have five yuan," the woman with the ponytail pleaded, trying to catch his gaze.

"Two for six," the cook repeated and without looking at her ladled more batter on the hot griddle. The boy slid one pancake out of the bag and handed her the single pancake with two 1-yuan coins. He shrugged apologetically before turning to the next customer.

"Asshole," she said under her breath. Ordering directly from the boy would have been a better strategy, she reasoned, but then the taste of the hotcake swept away her anger.

Amidst a stream of elderly people she passed Park 97, California Club and Tuscany, all restaurants that in the mid-90s had been the vanguard of Shanghai's current boom. With a straight back like a dancer's the woman passed a low fence behind which were a sun-bleached caterpillar ride and a grungy, inflated kiddie castle. A few older folks at small metal tables sipped tea from glass jars, smoked and chatted. She looked around to find a tea vendor to no avail, so she just rubbed the two coins in her pocket and moved on.

After the hotcake she felt better than she had in a while. She was also invigorated by the awareness that many approving eyes rested on her. She was by far the youngest *Tai Chi* instructor who offered morning lessons in Fuxing Park. Yang style, Wu, San, sword and staff: At one point or another she had trained with most of the groups that gathered here on weekend mornings. She briefly lifted her palms to acknowledge another *Shifu* whose serene countenance was topped with white hair whipped into mischievous wisps. Anybody could be a *Shifu* in the small hours of the morning, if they only bothered to stake a corner of the park and begin to move; nobody was checked for pedigree or title. If students showed up, the lone figure was instantly a teacher. But neither students nor *Shifu* were bound to stay together. Anybody who wanted to study could start training near a self-appointed master. But if the chosen *Shifu* did not acknowledge a student for weeks, or months, or years, even if no one else ever showed up in rain or shine, there was nowhere to complain. You simply started mimicking his moves, and maybe after a long while the *Shifu* deigned you worthy of a correction.

She had attached herself over the years to various *Shifus* after Auntie first took her to the park. She had paid them in the park's underground currencies, including small amounts of cash but more often cigarettes, telephone cards, precious advice. When she started teaching she had initially all but disregarded her students' offerings. The teaching was just something that happened when folks had begun to ask her advice on a form, a stance, or on the right way to jab a sword. For her, the practice had never been a job. Practicing in the park calmed her in a way nothing else could these days, not even reading the Russian books to which she had devoted herself, in addition to martial arts, since the age of ten. Lately things had gotten tougher, and she had landed her current tiny room through a tip from one of her students. By now the small cash-filled envelopes passed to her after teaching had become her only source of income.

"Breathe!" she admonished herself to quiet the piercing pain in her stomach that the hotcake had calmed for only a minute. She inhaled and passed four women in crinkled sweatsuits who wielded red-tassled plastic swords with a grace and strength that belied their toy equipment and age.

"Good discipline," she thought.

Like a flock of pigeons breaking into flight a pack of paunchy men and permed women unfolded both arms in unison, lifted a foot, turned, and with an unexpected explosive strike brought their arms and foot down swiftly. She had trained with them as a teenager, over ten years ago when the park had not yet been ringed by high-rises. The group's twenty-odd pairs of eyes were fastened on the movements of a purple-robed *Shifu* in the front. For an instant a few glances got caught on her figure, and a flutter passed through the group like a breeze passing over trees. Just as quickly the group's gaze settled back into the ancient order of movements that harked back to a time in Henan province long, long ago when the thought of a young woman *Shifu* would have resulted in hilarity, disdain, or death.

Her thoughts tightened around a worry that even her breathing could not suppress. She was expecting her landlord to show up at the park today. She did not want to see him, and yet she needed desperately to get another stay on paying the rent. She shook her fingers and cracked her knuckles, hard, to rid herself of the thought. Her stomach was clamoring for more food. Her last meal had been a bag of crackers she had slipped into her sleeve at a Larson's, followed by a cup of yogurt that a tourist had left on a table at the Starbucks near her house last night.

She took a deep breath, convincing herself for an instant that the park's fresh air could sate her. For a few steps she did nothing but inhale and exhale, and the earth continued to spin with her while she allowed herself to be carried forward by nothing but the will to be still. But then she suddenly lost track of the breathing and heard her own footsteps pounding hungry, hungry, hungry on the stone.

He's not here, she registered with a sharp pang of both relief and panic near a small lake. A school of orange-and-white koi now gathered close to the inky surface near the spot where she had put her bag on a smooth rock, their gulping mouths hankering for food. It would have been a peaceful, even serene moment, with the sun just reaching the tips of the pine trees by the pond, and the park filled with people lost in their deeply focused movements. But she looked around anxiously, hoping for, while at the same time dreading, the sight of him.

For a moment she willed herself to be still and relaxed, like a heron by the water's edge before it suddenly sets off in majestic flight. And this is what she did now: another breath and she took off, plunging into a sequence of movements at once so elegant and powerful that her hunger pangs and worries, her pride, anxiety and fear were all cast behind on the pavement like her velvet jacket and the bag with the threadbare lining that she had purchased in long-gone, better days.

She snapped her wrists and instantly her hands pointed like two drawn blades toward the pond, the fingers sharply together and the thumbs curled in. Two quick steps snatched from the tango, her hips smooth like melting ice and then her body stilled into a warrior pose at once taut and flexible like a willow. Mixing ballroom dancing and ancient *Tai Chi* chuan she had forged her own martial art, an unorthodox and perhaps even unholy amalgamation. She now faced a cluster of ornamental rocks set amidst windmill palms and tightly pruned shrubs. She willed herself to only look inward, to see none of this. *Yi-, er-, san-,* she aligned her mind with the rhythm of her movements. *Yi-, er-, san-, si-* . . . The gaggle of men and women that had gathered behind her breathed with her and now mirrored her moves.

* * *

She relied on her muscle memory to escape the anxious expectation of him showing up. But she did not clear her mind of all thought. Instead she reached back to the moment when she had set on her current path, the moment during a 1985 class trip to Beijing when she had been touched in a way that lifted her from the humdrum existence lived by everyone around her. Her mind returned to that day as it had so many times while she flowed through her movements, settling on that instant when she had been chosen from the crowd.

* * *

"You'll be able to travel to Beijing on a bus," Shuyu's mother had encouraged her ten-year old daughter. "In Beijing you'll see the leaders of our country, and also meet children from other schools."

"I don't want to go without you," Shuyu had sobbed.

Mother consoled her. "We'll get you a new red silk handkerchief for the trip, and I'll find special barrettes for your hair. Your cousin is also going and she'll ride on the same bus. The district leader chose you because Father has done so much to improve your school," Mother said.

That morning she had helped Daddy weed a lot behind their apartment house where neighbors hung their laundry to dry. He had also attached a piece of wire to lock the metal door, and with great effort had torn out a prickly bush that had grown in a cracked wall.

"Yes, *Meimei*, this trip is very special," Father had explained. "It's a privilege to represent your school, and neither Mother nor I have ever traveled to Beijing. We want you to remember everything and tell us about it when you return."

Shuyu swallowed hard.

"Thank you," she said to Father but then quickly looked away, afraid that she might start to cry again. A privilege? She wasn't sure what that meant. But she sensed that by not going she would disappoint them.

"*Meimei*, it will be fine," Father said and reached out to hug her. "Mommy will make special cakes and Cousin will look after you."

She felt better after Father hugged her, and by the time Mother crammed a small basket with hard-boiled eggs and flat bread under a seat on the bus, Shuyu was excited, if still nervous. She tightened her meticulously done braids.

"Tell me about everything you see, *Meimei*," Mother said and joined the waving parents outside. She held up four fingers of her right hand with the thumb against her palm to indicate the four days Shuyu would be gone.

"How many nights is four days?" Shuyu asked but before she could hear Mother's response the bus had pulled away.

They arrived late in Beijing and were shepherded into a gymnasium filled with metal cots. Shuyu wrapped herself in the thin sleeping bag and, clutching the new handkerchief she would wear the following day, she muffled her sobs and finally drifted to sleep.

The next morning the students visited a factory to

marvel at the industriousness of the capital's citizens. In a clean-swept courtyard the students sang for a workers' brigade. In the afternoon they rehearsed with students from another elementary school.

Finally, on the third day, the students were instructed to wear the new uniforms that had been stored in boxes in the bus's back row.

"Pick up a new shirt and put it on after breakfast," a teacher announced. "Do not spill any food on it! Then take your bags. We will leave directly for Shanghai after the ceremony."

At breakfast a girl sat down next to Shuyu in the huge, round cafeteria.

"Today we're not going to have a bathroom break for the whole day," the girl said with a knowing air.

"If you drink your tea now you'll have to pee but the bus will not stop for you," she continued. "And we'll have to stand for a long time during the ceremony without a break."

"What is a ceremony?" Shuyu asked, and added, "Can I eat the noodles?" Her eyes opened wide with worry. She instantly felt that she had to go to the bathroom. What if she had to pee while on the bus? She put her bowl back on the table.

"The ceremony is where we have to sing for the country's leaders," the girl replied, rolling her eyes. "What do you think we came here for?"

"But there must be bathrooms at the ceremony?" Shuyu asked.

"Hurry up and pick up your uniforms," a teacher's loud voice interrupted them. "Hurry! Hurry! Students from Junior School, finish your breakfast!"

Shuyu had not touched her tea or her bowl of noodles. She quickly got up from the table and hurried toward the doors. When Shuyu glanced back she saw the other girl pick up her bowl, drink the broth and run past her with a smirk.

Realizing that she had been tricked, Shuyu shouted, "You stole my breakfast!"

"Move along!" a teacher snapped and rapped Shuyu on the back of her head. "Everyone is waiting for you! You're going to make us late!"

Shuyu quickly slipped through the doors, picked up her uniform jacket and dragged her heavy bag on the bus. She found a spot next to a boy who took up nearly the whole seat. At least it was not the girl who had tricked her out of breakfast! She was thirsty but tried not to think about it, instead staring at the throng of bicycles through which the bus now pushed its way. She felt as if she already had to pee. When the bus finally stopped a woman in a grey suit got on.

"It's important that you stay with your teacher! Find a partner and line up outside, quickly! The delegation will arrive shortly, and you'll have to be on the stage before they get there."

"What is the delegation?" Shuyu asked a boy next to her but he did not respond. His hand was grimy so Shuyu touched it only with her pinky while they lined up. Then her grade was led across a big square where many people were waiting behind a cordon of soldiers. The students climbed a few steps on to a plywood stage. When Shuyu saw all of the people and rows of pots holding pretty red flowers lining the stage, she felt a surge of excitement. She tightened her braids and pushed up the gold barrettes. On the stage were soldiers and men and women in dark blue jackets, and

Shuyu noticed a large red and orange silk flower on Teacher's jacket. She strained to look past the taller children. Where is the delegation? she thought, and imagined an imperious person like Headmaster, or the foreman in Mother's factory who sprayed saliva when he spoke, emerging from among the soldiers.

"The Emperor of the Russian Empire is coming," a girl whispered but Shuyu kept her eyes focused on the student in front of her. She did not want to be tricked again.

"It's his first time in China, and the older students will sing in Russian," the girl continued.

"Do we have to sing in Russian, too?" Shuyu whispered, her eyes wide with worry.

"No, only the older kids sing in Russian," another girl said. "We sing the songs we rehearsed."

The girls fell quiet. Silently Shuyu mouthed the lines of the first song they had practiced for weeks, and relaxed a bit. Just then the woman in the grey dress pointed at her through the rows of students.

"You, little girl with the braids!" she called out. "Quick, come down here! Hurry up!"

Shuyu stared straight ahead. She kept mouthing the words to her song in an effort to ignore the woman. Without looking in the woman's direction Shuyu tried to spot Teacher to find out what to do. Then another girl nudged her hard.

"She's called for you!" the girl hissed. "What are you waiting for?"

Before Shuyu could respond, the girl pushed her again. She had to take a quick step not to fall, and then nearly tumbled through the students to the front of the stage.

"Come with me!" the woman whispered hoarsely and clutched Shuyu's hand hard. "Another student fell ill and you'll have to hand this bouquet to the General Secretary's wife."

Shuyu found herself next to a boy in a worker's cap who held a spray of yellow woodruff with pine branches.

"Take this," the woman handed Shuyu a large bouquet of red carnations tied with a white ribbon.

Shuyu cradled the flowers in her arms just like the boy held his bouquet. Shuyu wanted to tell the woman to pick another girl when everyone suddenly fell silent. Among several people in dark suits and more soldiers who ascended the stage Shuyu glimpsed a Western man with a maroon spot on his head. A loud voice boomed from the speaker in front of Shuyu but she could not understand what was being said. She glimpsed Teacher and tried to catch his attention, hoping to be put back among the students in her grade who had now begun to sing their song, but his face was tight like a locked door. The song finished and the boy walked across the stage. Someone nudged Shuyu in the back so she couldn't do anything but follow him.

"Give your flowers to the Caucasian woman," Shuyu heard someone say urgently. Several soldiers parted and with the crowd's applause surging around her Shuyu looked at a white woman with reddish hair.

"How beautiful!" Shuyu thought. "Like the paper lantern by Grandma's bed!"

When the boy handed his flowers to the man with the red mark Shuyu thrust her bouquet toward the white lady, but someone else took them from Shuyu's hand before she could reach her. Shuyu tore her gaze from the woman's big eyes. She quickly tried to curt-sy, for a moment unsure which leg to put forward although she had practiced with Mother many times, and turned.

"Devochka," Shuyu heard a gentle voice. "Devoch-ka," the voice repeated, like the hua mei bird Grandfather kept in a small bamboo cage.

Shuyu stopped and stared at the plywood floorboards, grinning broadly with embarrassment. In a stern voice, as if Shuyu had done something wrong, a Chinese woman said something to the white lady. Shuyu did not know whether to follow the boy off the stage or stay and listen. Then the Chinese woman asked in a voice that made Shuyu think she was being reprimanded, "How old are you?"

Shuyu didn't know what to say. The Chinese woman looked at her with a furrowed brow, as if she was about to yell at her. But the lady with the bright reddish hair smiled warmly at her and had raised her eyebrows slightly, as if waiting for an answer.

Her eyes sparkled from deep within their brown centers, as if a star had plunged into the ocean. There was no more Teacher, no more soldiers and no more men in suits. Shuyu found herself alone on the stage with the lantern lady as if she had been plucked from her class and transported to a spot very far away. Shuyu saw nothing but the peculiar glow of the woman's hair, and kindness in those deep brown eyes. Grinning drunk-happy ear-to-ear she was alone in them while the woman smiled.

The soldiers had formed a circle around the woman, the girl, and the interpreter, around the Chinese officials with the party insignia on their lapels, and around the man with the maroon mark on his head a few feet away. The man who had first spoken into the microphone clasped his hands behind his back and looked on impassively.

"How old are you?" the Chinese woman asked again.

"Nine years," Shuyu responded but realized that the white lady did not understand. She repeated her answer, more loudly. Then she looked down and noticed that under the dark skirted suit and white blouse the woman wore gold shoes. Her smile got wider yet.

"Gold shoes! They are so beautiful." She burst out over the Chinese interpreter while pointing at the shoes.

The lady said something in her gentle voice.

"These are nice hair clips you have," the Chinese woman sharply addressed Shuyu, again as if she had done something wrong.

Shuyu lifted her eyes up at the white woman.

"Mother gave them to me," she responded.

"May I see them?" the interpreter asked after the lady had said something else. Shuyu now grasped how the interpreter worked. She took out a barrette but her eyes darted back to the gold shoes. "They must be very expensive," she thought.

The shoes had rounded toes and the woman's feet looked smooth and cool in them, as if she could walk all day through hot summer streets without getting tired. Mother had once borrowed a pair of fancy brown shoes from Auntie when Father had received an award but that night she had soaked her feet in warm water because they had been too tight.

"Your shoes are so beautiful," Shuyu blurted out

and pointed at the shoes. She quickly clasped her mouth but the Russian lady laughed. Then, to Shuyu's astonishment, she reached down and removed her left shoe with one hand and, balancing on her right gold-shimmering heel on the plywood stage, extended it toward Shuyu.

Shuyu did not dare breathe. "It's so light! Like a tiny bird."

The lady waited for the interpreter to translate and laughed again. She steadied herself with one hand on the lectern while balancing on one leg, and ignored that the entire delegation, including her husband and the Chinese officials, waited near the stairs.

"Did you braid your hair by yourself today?" the interpreter translated from the Russian that cascaded over Shuyu. "Why did you choose gold barrettes to tie back the braids?"

"I braided my hair by myself but Mother bought these barrettes for the trip," Shuyu answered. She extricated one of the clasps from one braid.

When the woman put her golden shoe back on the interpreter hissed at Shuyu.

"Leave your hair alone," she snapped at Shuyu with unveiled frustration. "The Party Secretary has to leave."

Raisa Gorbachev reached out and helped Shuyu untangle a strand of hair from the clasp. For a fleeting moment Shuyu's hand touched the white woman's cool fingers. The woman's laugh trickled down Shuyu's neck and spine. Shuyu could not help from joining in that laughter while the soldiers and the men looked on stoically.

"Spasiba," the lady said.

The interpreter grimly remained silent.

Shuyu smiled at the lantern lady. "Put it in your hair!"

Then she waited, stunned at her own audacity but also feeling as if there really was nobody besides her and the lady on the stage. Shuyu gestured at the woman's reddish bob.

The woman raised her finely drawn eyebrows. "Ahh," she let out and carefully clipped the barrette around a few wisps of her hair. There it hung like a shiny dragonfly balancing on a thin twig. The lady smiled and turned toward the group of men. She cocked her head, touched her hair with one hand and pursed her lips. The man with the red splotch smiled with his eyes but his face stayed immobile. He briefly waved toward the students, took a heavy step down the stairs and disappeared from Shuyu's view.

"You should not have spoken to her," the flushed Chinese interpreter reprimanded Shuyu. "This was the Russian Party Secretary's Wife! Raisa Gorbachev! She does not have time for little girls. Who is your teacher?"

But then someone called for the interpreter who rushed after the delegation, and Shuyu was caught in the throng of students now waiting to exit the stage. She took each step carefully, imagining a finely woven golden shoe on each foot instead of her plain brown student shoes. And truly, by the time she reached the bus she felt as if she were not walking but gliding on air, buoyed by the encounter with the lantern lady.

Shuyu ignored Teacher's order to hold another student's hand. "Look," she wanted to say, "the lantern lady took one of my barrettes, and let me hold her shoe. I held her golden shoe!"

"What did Raisa Gorbachev say to you?" Teacher asked.

"Who?" Shuyu responded.

"This was Raisa Gorbachev, Russia's most important lady," Teacher explained. "Raisa Gorba-chev."

"Rai-sa? Rai-sa?" Shuyu tried pronouncing the name. "Raisa. It's beautiful." She walked on without responding to Teacher. "Raisa."

Shuyu's cheeks glowed. She shook off another girl's hand and climbed aboard the bus all by herself. She undid her braids and let the hair cover her face. Thus veiled from the other kids' view she leaned her forehead against the window.

"Raisa," she mouthed softly. "I will call myself Raisa from now on."

* * *

When Shuyu alighted in Shanghai early the next morning Mother shrieked with worry.

"What happened to your hair?" she cried out. "You look like you fell!"

Shuyu did not respond.

"I want you to call me Raisa from now on," she said while Mother smoothed down her hair. "I will not respond to Shuyu any longer."

And that was that. From that day on ten-year old Shuyu refused to respond to her given name. She had been touched by something when Raisa Gorbachev took the barrette from her hair, and no longer considered herself just another little girl.

"I met the wife of the General Secretary of the Central Committee of the Union of Soviet Republics," she announced proudly to Teacher after listening carefully to Grandfather's explanations the night before. "I will call myself Raisa from now on."

"Your name is your name, Shuyu," Teacher responded. "Sit down! You've missed three days of school and will have to work hard to keep up."

Her parents tried to reason with her. But they quickly learned that if they wanted their daughter to hear them at all they had to use her new Russian name, "Raisa," which meant they had lost the argument before they could make their case.

"Shuyu," Father said, "you cannot simply choose a name, and an odd one that is hard to pronounce at that. We chose your name because it will set you on a good path in life. One of your aunties is named Shuyu and she has an important job in her hometown."

"My name is Raisa," the girl responded.

"But the wrong name can be unlucky!" Mother said.

"A name must be right for a person's birthday, *Meimei*," Father explained. "The wrong name can weigh down your life. What will your teachers say?"

Only Grandfather supported her. "It's a great honor that Russia's first lady spoke with you," he said. "When I studied in Moscow the Russians were kind. It is a good omen for your life."

Carefully he drew two characters that sounded like Raisa on a piece of paper which she attached to the wall.

"No child should pick her own name," Grandmother interjected.

"Shush," Grandfather silenced his wife. "The girl's life will be special. She met the General Secretary's wife!"

Although they struggled to pronounce the new name, not one of her classmates made fun of her. Raisa moved through school with an air of indifference, friendly enough with the other kids but no longer part of them. Soon even the teachers were chastened by the young girl's resolve, or they just stopped worrying about one girl in a class of thirty-seven. Raisa had left her name behind like the yellow comforter under which she had slept as a baby, or the small slate-board with the sponge on a string from first grade that she had abandoned once she started using a fountain pen.

In fact, Raisa's parents were intimidated by the change that had come over her daughter. They sat up nights with the apartment door open to the hallway light and discussed the change they perceived in their daughter.

"She does better in school now," Father tried to calm Mother.

"But we hardly know what she does!" Mother said, exasperated. "A few days ago she told me that she's been studying Russian on her own. Russian! A student should listen to her teachers and not decide for herself what to study."

Each night after dinner Raisa rinsed her stockings and then carefully pinned them to the clean parts of the bamboo drying rack outside the kitchen window. In the mornings she brushed and braided her hair, dressed quickly in clothes she laid out the night before, and just as rapidly finished breakfast. Then she used the few minutes before Grandfather walked her to school to study Russian grammar. Except for a stern sentence noting the futile measures taken by the school to let Raisa use her given name, her report card teemed with excellents.

To her parents it seemed as if Raisa did not need them any more. Of course there were tasks she had not mastered; she was only ten. But she exuded an uncanny confidence as if there was nothing in her path that she couldn't conquer. She had been touched by someone special, and she now pursued a direction separate from her classmates that was dictated by the gold slippers she had seen on the lantern woman's feet.

"*Meimei* needs the exercise because she studies too much," Auntie had insisted when she saw Raisa early one morning with her face buried in the Russian primer. "It's not good for girls to be too bookish," she announced and from then on took her niece for *Tai Chi* chuan lessons in Fuxing Park.

*   *   *

After high school Raisa had enrolled in a technical college and then found work as a Russian interpreter. For a few years she earned enough money to rent her own room. But she worked only as much as she needed, in addition to Grandfather's humble monthly contribution, to cover necessities. Whenever she could pilfer a free moment, after *Tai Chi* in the morning and the hours translating legal documents or interpreting for business visitors, she devoted herself to rendering the Russian literary classics into Chinese. She puzzled over the right Chinese expression for Pushkin's –

"We shall all go down under the eternal vaults.
Someone's hour is already at hand."

– until satisfied by yoking the Russian "vaults" under the Chinese tian, for heaven.

"My translation of Pushkin was published in a Beijing magazine," she shouted over the din of evening rush hour into an orange telephone receiver at her apartment complex's guard station, thrilled at seeing her name in print.

"How much did you get paid?" Mother shouted back from her end of the line, her voice thin and echoing. Mother and Father had moved back to their hometown with the money from a developer who bought their apartment building in Shanghai.

"It's Pushkin," Raisa responded excitedly, "this is my first publication!"

"When are you getting married?" Mother responded. Father began to say something but Raisa had already hung up and with a tight face paid the attendant for the call.

Then the interpreting business dried up.

"We're just not getting requests right now," the manager at the translation firm had said on the day Raisa had returned from Grandfather's funeral, her bag heavy with the books he had left behind. "What about the mining company?" Raisa asked urgently. "They said they would return for negotiations soon."

"They haven't returned our calls," the man responded. "Most of the briefs are written in English now."

"I'm the best Russian interpreter you've got," Raisa said, "and they've always liked my work."

The man ignored the edge in her voice. "Perhaps you could try private tutoring," he suggested. "There's just no demand for Russian now."

*　*　*

"Try to learn English," a friend had recommended a few days later at Fang's Café. The friend was friendly with one of the waiters and called him over.

"Zhu teaches English," she said by way of introduction. "He makes good money at *English First!*, and they're always looking for teachers."

The waiter was silent.

"Hmmmm," Raisa nodded her head.

When the waiter had walked back to the counter she blurted out at her friend, "I can't do it! I cannot sit in an English class with a bunch of obnoxious high school students and teach that bubble-gummy language. Really, I am not a spoiled brat but I can't do it! Russian is the language of the soul. If I study English now I'll lose all of the Russian that I worked for years to learn. If I now start doing something else I'll never finish my translation of Doctor Zhivago."

"Of course," Raisa's friend said while trying not to show her exasperation. "You've worked hard, and I know you're very good. But I think once you've learned English you'll be able to pay rent and still be able to translate for Dr. Zhi Wa Go."

"It's not a doctor, it's a book," Raisa burst out. "This is precisely the problem! Nobody here knows the great works of Russian literature, and instead people want to do business in English. There's nothing worth translating from English."

Her friend was silent.

"I know you're trying to help," Raisa said more calmly, "it's just that after so many years of hard work I won't be able to stay in Shanghai!" Her eyes filled with tears. "All I want is to work on these translations! I live in a tiny room, I buy no clothes, I hardly eat! Why can't I stay here, near the big libraries and translate these Russian books? If I give up now none of them will never appear in Chinese!"

"I know you've worked hard. Have you spoken with your landlord?" her friend asked.

"Ugh, please," Raisa blurted out. "I can't stand him. I've helped him with some work with these Russian business guys so he's been okay about the rent."

"Maybe he has more work for you?" her friend inquired.

"He wants to take *Tai Chi* lessons, too. If I get a few more rich clients to study *Tai Chi* maybe I can cover the rent and work on my Russian translations."

"That's a great idea!" her friend ventured. "You've learned so much *Tai Chi Chuan*, and especially foreigners are into martial arts now. You could teach them." She gestured with her head toward the waiter near the counter. "That waiter earns enough money teaching English to work on his own art projects."

"Who are you kidding?" Raisa responded scornfully. "I heard that guy gets paid by a rich lady who picks him up after work. Look at the tattoo on his arm! He's just weird."

"He is studying at the television academy to design his own programs. I think he's good-looking!" Raisa's friend said defensively.

"Oh my god, you like him!" Raisa said, astonished, and laughed.

"I do not!" her friend responded brusquely and pulled on her coat. "Anyway, he's just a friend. Well, I think you should definitely find more students to teach *Tai Chi*," she concluded. And to get back at Raisa for making fun of the waiter, she added before walking away, "Without learning English I can't see how you'll be able to stay in Shanghai."

* * *

For the past few weeks Raisa had racked her brain for a money-making scheme. Only now, this Sunday morning near the pond in Fuxing Park, her mind had come to be still in the center of her *Tai Chi* movements like a spider waiting in its web.

"*Yi-, er-,*" she counted but a thought interrupted her, "What if he doesn't show up?"

She succeeded to channel the flash of anger into the quick but precise movement of her arms.

"*Yi-, er-, san-,*" she started over but it lasted but a moment.

What if he didn't show up? What could she do? But to see that pig here, this one place where she could forget about her worries for a few minutes. Torn between disgust at the thought of seeing him and anger at being stood up, her mind tripped over itself like an unskilled fighter wielding two weapons at once.

Her eyes focused inward while her disciples mimicked her unique combination of ballroom dancing, step aerobics, and *Tai Chi*. Clad in black, moving gracefully, seemingly impervious to her surroundings: to everyone else Raisa was the undisputed and serene ruler of this corner of the park. When she started her routine the hua mei birds in bamboo cages brought by their owners seemed to quiet down, and even the sounds of Jay Chou tunes and big band classics blaring on nearby radios faded. A tourist stopped, snapped a picture, and then just watched, clearly astonished that this young woman commanded the attention of so many white-haired, wizened people.

Just at this instant Raisa glimpsed him by the pond. The sight cut through her like a small electric shock.

To regain her focus she stomped one of her boots on the ground. Her long ponytail bobbed with the movement and the women and men behind her quickly stomped as well, surprised by the unexpectedly forceful step.

The movements that followed a rhythm dating back centuries and that she had honed in years and years of practice were now aimed at the single goal of keeping him here in the park. He had lowered himself on to a nearby bench, wearing a shiny dark blue suit over an open-collared dress shirt and smoked a cigarette. His legs were spread to let his gut spill over his belt, and his trousers had slid up to reveal white calves.

He flicked his cigarette into the pond and leaned forward, intently watching the group of disciples following Raisa's every move. Abruptly, and without looking in his direction, Raisa broke her stance and walked up to the bench.

"I see you're up early today," she said, keeping her voice deliberately steady although the exercise had accelerated her breathing.

"You can keep on teaching," the man said and stared at her breasts. "It's very inspiring to watch. I'm having a good time here."

Raisa turned and walked back to the edge of the pond. She suddenly felt damp all over, furious at his rude comeback and angry at herself for not controlling her heaving chest. She resumed her pose and strained to blot out her awareness of his leering gaze.

She stretched her mind until she thought nothing but felt only her arms, her hands, her fingertips and every muscle and tendon along the way.

"In your mind," she thought to herself and threw a sharp punch.

"In – !

your – !

mind - !"

The act of thinking defied her effort to not think, to not be preoccupied with him. She remembered what she told her students often: be the water and the wave at once. Move powerfully without moving, be still when using the greatest force. Then she did not think but only moved and for that instant lost awareness of his gaze and let go of her anger and her shame. It lasted but a second.

She had worked so hard to live in Shanghai, and she had been frugal to the extreme! When her friends shopped for new clothes she had smiled indulgently at their extravagant taste, and saved her money for a good Chinese-Russian dictionary, good paper, and the postage to mail her translations to literary magazines in Beijing. She found ways of eating without any expense, by shoplifting in the big department store food sections that catered to foreigners, and even eating the half-finished fruit cups and rolls left by tourists in the Western fast-food joints. And she planned on paying her rent! That was why she had called him last night, to offer him *Tai Chi* lessons so that he would forgive her the back rent in lieu of payment. The thought of forking over money for that shit-hole where she slept each night, fearful of catching some disease from the dirty walls, made her angrier yet.

She broke off her routine, picked her bag up, and stood for a moment looking out over the small pond. She calmed her breathing and tried, deliberately, beginning with her forehead, then her eyes, her mouth, finally her neck to drain all expression. It was important to regain her focus. No time to be angry but to keep a cool mind.

She could feel the bulk of his body next to her.

"Wanna get breakfast?" he said and flicked another cigarette into the pond. A large goldfish snapped at it but quickly let go, which prompted the man to laugh.

"I asked the *ayi* to prepare food," he said. "The driver is waiting by the gate."

"I rode my bicycle here," Raisa said quietly and started to walk away from the pond. "I don't think I'll be able to come to your place this morning."

"You said on the phone last night I could take a lesson today," the man said. "My wife's traveling so it's a good day."

"It has to be short," Raisa responded, "I have to be somewhere." This was a lie, and her mind raced to think of how to keep him interested but not promise too much.

"You owe me four months of rent," the man stated coldly.

"Of course, Gao, I'll just have to get my bike." She slowed down just a bit and then, in a more conciliatory tone, "I just didn't think that you would bring the car. I'll ride the bike to your place. I'll come for one lesson but I won't have time for breakfast. And I'll stop by during the week to look over the Russian emails."

"Okay," the man agreed, "I'll meet you at my apartment."

On the way out of the park she tore open an envelope a student had handed her and took out two 10-yuan notes. She passed the cook behind the portable stove and briefly considered buying another pancake, but the thought that he hadn't been willing to discount the hotcakes earlier prompted her to walk past without so much as a glance. She felt Gao's eyes on her back and wanted to get out of his sight. By the time Raisa rode her bicycle through the empty streets she had regained her focus.

A few minutes later she locked her bike to a rack near a large apartment complex. "Two yuan!" demanded a woman with a leather purse strung across her chest. She pointed at the bikes on the sidewalk. "Parking fee."

Wordlessly, Raisa handed her two coins. But her mind was on what would happen next. She had to make this visit count.

As she crossed over a concrete zig-zag-shaped bridge leading to the front doors she remembered the belief that ghosts cannot turn corners. If this belief were true it would keep half the residents out of this buildings, she thought grimly as she reached the shiny lobby. Bloodsuckers one and all, she thought while briskly walking past the security guards toward the elevators, her head held high.

She tightened her ponytail and smoothed down her sweater in front of the elevator's mirrored doors. She tucked her belt under to hide a rubber band replacing a missing loop. Once in the elevator she lowered herself into a warrior stance, her palms lightly touching in front of her chest, while the cabin rose silently to the top floor. The elevator opened with a muted ding directly into the apartment's foyer. She was determined to make him believe that she would be back on her feet soon. Appearing desperate, she had learned long ago, was a sure-fire way to turn off help. Only when she brimmed with confidence and appeared completely self-sufficient, she had learned long ago, were people willing to help.

"Come here," the man's voice bellowed out from an adjacent room.

Raisa crossed the marble floor and entered a large, carpeted room. She was as focused as she had ever been, her mind and body intent on getting the back rent dismissed and perhaps a loan from Gao. Gao was sprawled on a large blue leather sofa in front of a wall covered with several huge, steel-framed mirrors. On the opposite side loomed a massive desk with a dark blue leather top, blue leather chairs, a flat-screen monitor and an exercise machine.

"Here, here," he said and patted the cushions next to him.

"We should start class right away," Raisa said, staying on her side of the enormous white and gold coffee table in front of the couch. "We should start with breathing exercises, and then we can work on the second form."

"Yeah, let's breathe together," the man said and laughed.

Raisa bit her lips. "Do you want to take a class or not?" she asked.

"Sure, sure," the man responded, "don't get upset. Remember that you called me!"

The *ayi* walked into the room and placed a tray with steamers, bowls of congee, shelled peanuts in thin maroon skins, pickled sliced daikon, chopped eggs and bowls with spices next to fried dough sticks twisted into braids. A western-style silver carafe and several bone-white cups sat next to two bowls of steaming soup. Raisa eyed the meal hungrily but made an effort to betray nothing on her face. The *ayi* poured soy milk into a glass and topped it with diet coke from a can. When the whitish foam ran over she quickly wiped off the glass and tray.

"Get out!" the man snapped and flicked his hand in her direction. "Don't come back till you're called!"

The *ayi* hurried from the room, and the man turned to Raisa.

"You wanna eat?"

"No, thank you," Raisa said, her eyes devouring each morsel on the tray.

She worried that her stomach might grumble but was determined to make him beg her to accept anything.

The man sipped from the foamy drink and picked up a dumpling with his chopsticks.

"You're sure?" he asked but did not wait for an answer. "All right," he said and lifted himself off the couch. "I got some business people stopping by in a while. Let's do the class."

He placed one hand on Raisa' left hip and with the other reached for her right breast. She pushed his arms away roughly, angrily.

"Gao, let's do the class!" she snapped. "That's what I'm here for."

If he paid today, she quickly calculated in her head, and forgave her some of the rent against the promise of future classes, she would stand him up next week.

Make him beg her, rather than the other way around. Then she felt a sharp pain in her stomach and did not know whether it was from hunger or rage. Only the thought of promising Gao another appointment and then standing him up made her feel a little better. She took a step away from Gao next to the coffee table.

"Breathe deeply," she instructed him, "bend your left knee and lower yourself into the pose." It was as much a directive to herself as to him.

For a short while Gao followed directions. She extended her arm very quickly and then settled deep into a low warrior pose: he closely mimicked each move. For his bulk Gao displayed surprising agility

"Drop your shoulders," Raisa guided him. "Don't raise them when lifting your arms."

"Hmm," Gao groaned but followed her instructions carefully. After a few minutes he plopped down on the blue couch.

"Come sit down," he ordered and patted the couch again. "It's too strenuous."

"You'll soon find it easier," said Raisa and remained on her feet. "I'll show you the next form."

"Come here, I said." He patted the couch. "I'll show you the next form."

Raisa sat down on the edge of the large coffee table, only a few feet away from the food that was now getting cold.

"I could make you a baby, you know," the man said.

She felt another pang in her abdomen.

"Gao, what are you saying? How can I have a baby right now?" she said, rattled by his suggestion and trying to calculate her response. "I have no money for food, and I owe you a few months of rent."

"If you have my child I'll pay for everything. You know I can afford it."

He extended his hand and tried again to touch her. Raisa leaned back slightly on the coffee table, making it look as if she was just finding a more comfortable perch but really to escape his reach.

"Raisa, you know what I want," Gao said. He unbuttoned his shirt with the monogrammed cuffs, wriggled out of it and dropped it on the floor. His white belly and chest shone with sweat.

"Gao, I want something with you but now is not a good time. I need to finish a few projects, and get more work. I want something in the future but I need time." She swallowed hard to keep from retching and watched his face closely, gauging his reaction.

"You want to be with me because of me, or because of the rent?" he said.

"Because of you but I also need to figure out the rent," she responded.

"Take off your sweater," he said.

"Gao, let's go back to the lesson," she responded.

"Get over here!" he retorted sharply. "You know this is what I want. You called me last night! I'm the boss!"

He scrambled to his feet with surprising speed. "What do you think you're doing? Either you're very naïve, or you're even more calculating than I thought."

"Gao, we were going to practice *Tai Chi!*" Raisa said, her voice very controlled. "You know this has been a hard time for me these past couple of months."

"You know why you came over here!" he responded, hoarse with anger. "You know damn well what I want, and you're obviously here for a reason!"

Gao leaned over again and this time she did not pull back. Completely immobile she inhaled and closed her eyes, relying on the breathing techniques she had learned in years of *Tai Chi*. With the next deep breath she reached back, back through the ancient traditions to find refuge somewhere inside of her, to find a place of tranquility and peace far beyond his touch.

"Don't move," she thought to herself and willed her body not to flinch. "I'll let him only go so far." She could feel a film of sweat forming on her chest, and along her neck and back.

Her body rose on its own accord from the coffee table next to the tray loaded with food while she continued to negotiate.

"Gao, it's not a good time for me right now. Maybe later we can be together but with the rent and everything, it's really hard for me to think about being with anyone."

"You have a boyfriend? Is that it?" he said, growing more impatient.

"No, no, I told you I'm really not in a position to be with anyone right now. It's not about you."

He got up quickly and this time she did not pull back. They were on the blue couch. She closed her eyes and tried to shut her mind, too, so at least she would not know but only feel – body-feel but not feel in her mind, not know – his touch.

"*Yi-, er-, san-, si-,*" she formed the numbers soundlessly and willed her breathing into the rhythm of the count. Her body settled into the counting and took her mind with it. Nearly one thousand years ago monks had developed the forms on which Raisa relied now, after Damo had withdrawn to a cave high up on Mt.

Song, to revive their limbs after hours of meditation. In this ornately furnished room atop a brand-new Shanghai housing complex Raisa now turned inside out this ancient technique. With each number she tried to flee the physical sensation of her own body, make it senseless and numb to Gao's touch so close.

"*Wu-, liu-, chi-, ba-,*" she counted, willing herself into a space as far from the world as the cave where Damo had meditated with such intensity that his image had been burned onto the walls. But Raisa's reflection flashed not on the walls of a protective cave to inspire disciples. Instead her reflection was caught in Gao's gaudy mirrors, a body frozen with desperation and rage held in check by her breath. She murmured the numbers and was transported back to the park with Auntie instructing her, back to some of the yellow-toothed *Shifus* who had praised her talent, back to the time when the world had seemed to applaud and assist her every move.

His hands, his body, his lips and mouth and everything were on her.

She thought, "don't throw up," and pressed her mouth shut. "Only this far."

"*Yi-, er-, san-,*" she murmured. She started over again, "*Yi-, er- . . .*"

With her counting she fought him, fought against the shame and the outrage and against feeling him so close. She heard his panting and the sound of a dish crashing on the floor, and she heard the sound of their bodies against the smooth leather of the couch. Then she heard nothing but the counting in a spot inside of her where nothing else took place.

And then suddenly Gao was sprawled like an oversized bug on the plush rug with the blue chrysanthe-mum pattern, his white torso glistening with sweat and his face contorted in anger and pain.

He clutched his side with both hands.

"How dare you! You know why I asked you over here," he spat on the expensive carpet while struggling to get up. He clutched his side. "And now this!"

She stared silently at Gao and realized only after a few seconds that she stood in full warrior pose, one leg back and one fist chambered tightly by her side. Her right arm was extended straight out in front, with her palm sideways and its edge facing him. "Wu zhi pin long," passed through her mind, "'five fingers together as one.'" Auntie's *Shifu* had drilled the saying into her, and make her practice hitting the sides of trees, street signs, walls, her bedpost, until she could tighten her hand into a steel blade.

She raised herself up and now Gao looked not so much angry as defeated. He rubbed a large red spot on his side.

"Come on, Raisa," he pleaded. "I couldn't help my-self!"

He sounded like a little boy who had been denied a treat.

Raisa cleared her throat. It was hard to breathe.

"Gao, I have to leave," she said and took her velvet jacket off the coffee table.

"Just wait a moment! I'll make it up to you!" he pleaded in what sounded like a stifled wail. "I have something I want to give you! I'll be only a minute."

He bent down with a groan to pick his shirt off the floor. A red welt had formed on his side.

"Wait just a second!" he disappeared through a mirrored door recessed into the wall.

With a sudden burst of fury Raisa pushed and used all her strength to shove the blue couch against the mirrored door. She pushed again to make the top of the couch flush with the brass door handles shaped liked flying cranes. It looked as if the heavy, ugly piece of furniture had been in this spot since the Qing Dynasty. The room was calm again, its blue furniture and thick rug settled like the sky after a brief but violent storm.

She rushed toward the desk and rifled through Gao's jacket. Seconds later she tore open the doors to the closet in the marble-floored foyer. After a quick glance she took a large leather bag from a shelf holding dozens of purses and totes, quietly closed the door, and darted across the entryway to a side door near the elevators. At the door she paused briefly. She rushed back to the hallway closet and re-emerged, now clutching two bags.

Once out of the wood-paneled foyer everything was dirty cinderblock, harsh neon lights, and unpainted cement stairs. The narrow space practically shook with the roaring from the elevator engines and air conditioning units a few feet above her head. She rushed down several flights, careful not to trip and fall, and then slowed down to stuff the bundle of banknotes she had taken from Gao's jacket into the leather bag.

"That's it, you pig!" she said and continued to hurry down the stairs. "That's it! 'I'm the boss!'" she disgustedly imitated Gao's voice, trying to laugh.

At the bottom of the stairs she pushed open a heavy metal door to the service basement. Quickly she walked past a garbage-sorting room filled to the ceiling with boxes, bags, bundles of newspapers and plastic jugs.

She pulled her hair out of the ponytail and slipped the barrette into the bag.

By the time she emerged into the neighboring building's lobby from the service door, she had regained her focus. She suddenly remembered the day she had met Raisa Gorbachev, and how she had learned that afternoon in Beijing that the world would see her in ways that had little to do with who she really was. She almost smiled at the memory of meeting Raisa Gorbachev, seeing in her mind the little girl with the braids who had not yet realized that she would be able to contribute to the world through her gifted translations.

Let the doormen see what they want, she thought when passing the lobby desk with her head high and not even a glance in the guards' direction. What they beheld was not Raisa, not a broke and desperate translator of Russian who had found her mission in life through a chance encounter with Raisa Gorbachev nearly twenty years ago. No, what they saw was just another rich tenant who you'd better respect lest her asshole of a husband report you to the supervisor. Raisa moved her head to make her long hair swing, and haughtily ignored the bellman's greeting while exiting through the revolving doors. Make them see what they want to see: another spoiled Shanghai wife going out to shop. Outside, in the balmy morning air, the rage that had prompted her to imprison Gao with his own blue couch only minutes earlier settled like leaves at the bottom of a cold canteen of tea.

She stepped out of a gate on a sidewalk where workers were tying emerald-green branches trimmed from plantain trees into quick-wilting bundles. She tucked the bags under her arm, unlocked her bike and pedaled swiftly, but not so fast as to arouse suspicion, to the new train station. Once there she walked away from the bike without bothering to lock it.

"This is a pay lot," an attendant called out and scribbled Raisa's arrival time on a tiny slip of paper. "You gotta pay!" the man raised his voice but Raisa ignored him and quickly caught up to the crowd pressing through the station's doors.

Inside she approached a stand where a woman cracked eggs on to paper-thin pancakes sprinkled with finely minced vegetables and meat. Raisa slipped a hand into the bag under her shoulder and extended a 100-yuan bill.

"Three pancakes, please," she said.

A cook from an adjacent stall leaned over, his eyes on the meat-red bill.

"Some dumplings? Vegetable? Pork? Beef? We also have soda cans or tea, and watermelon, very fresh."

"Pork," Raisa agreed and waited. "And beef!" she added after a moment.

Her mouth watered, and she rocked slightly on the balls of her feet in anticipation. Pork dumplings were her favorite, and she could not remember the last time she had tasted them fresh. The cooks slid three pancakes into a bag, nimbly filled two Styrofoam containers with dumplings, and added plastic containers with cubed watermelon and a bottle of green tea.

Raisa handed the cook the 100 yuan and walked away without waiting for the change.

"Lady!" the man ran after her to hand her the money but Raisa smiled and waved him off. With a puzzled look he slipped the note in his shirt and quickly returned to his cart. Raisa waited in line to buy a ticket and then entered the gated waiting area reserved for passengers.

"Beijing 11:04," she murmured to herself. In Beijing she would call on Cousin who worked at a tour agency. For years this woman had wanted Raisa to come up, and for years Raisa had insisted that the Shanghai Public Library was a better resource for her translation of the Russian classics. Now it was time to go.

She pushed her way on the train and found a seat next to a long-haired young man with an elaborately designed canvas bag. The young man took out a notebook and with abrupt little strokes began to sketch the rushing crowd in front of them. With her elbows wedged by her sides Raisa began to take small bites of the dumplings filled with seasoned meat. She chewed with her eyes closed. She took another bite, and held the food in her mouth and let its delicious taste flood through her body. When she was finished she carefully extricated a book from her own bag. Doctor Shivago, it said on the title in Cyrillic letters. She pulled out a book mark and opened a page marked up with Chinese characters in different colors in the margins. She could crack open the book only a bit in the narrow space on top of her thighs. The train started moving. After the conductor had checked her ticket Raisa carefully turned sideways, crammed in on both sides by other passengers, to reach inside the bag. She slowly raised one knee at a time to lift her stockinged feet out of her boots. Then she placed a pair of expensive-looking golden pumps on the floor. She had taken them from Gao's hallway closet. She slipped her feet into the golden shoes, pushed her boots deep under the seat, and for the first time in a long time felt as if she could float again.

BEGGAR'S CHICKEN

CONTROL

Zhu stood in his long-sleeved white teaching shirt between posters of a multi-turreted fairy-tale castle, deep green and cave-like forest clearings, and a row of cascading waterfalls. About an hour or so into his Saturday afternoon English class his pants were covered with yellow chalk where he'd wiped his hands. Most of the teenage boys squeezed behind the small desks were beginning to fade, and even the girls now batted their eyelids at their favorite tutor with fading regularity. At the back of the class the middle school students who used the rooms during the week had hung hand-painted versions of the same castles, forests, and waterfalls. A few parents huddled against this backdrop to ensure that Zhu paid enough attention to their precious offspring. They were not supposed to stay in class after the first two weeks of tutoring, but Zhu had learned to ignore their watchful presence.

Zhu learned most of his English in chatrooms for gaming sites, and although he'd never really heard the language spoken, he now earned enough as a language tutor at the *English First!* institute to cover his rent. He liked teaching and knew how to engage his students, playing on the boys' envy of his coveted status as a student at the Shanghai Film and Television Academy, and on the girls' generic infatuation with him as a young, hip, and unmarried teacher.

"I loved you," "I love you," "I will love you in

heaven," Zhu now intoned against the backdrop of Alpine villages and multihued natural wonders while pointing at the board. "Past, imperfect, present, future: Use a different color for each tense."

He called on individual students to decline the verbs written on the board in yellow chalk.

"I have loved I loved I love I will love . . ." "*Wo ai wo ai wo ai*" he recited for the teenagers.

"I have loved," "I loved," "I love," "I will love," the students repeated sleepily. Zhu bunched a shirtsleeve over his left hand and wiped several lines off the board. "Am," "was," "will be," was the students' response.

Pointing with a bamboo rod at the blackboard, Zhu asked them to read the tenses from an exercise he had typed up the night before: "My love will last," "I loved you once," "I shall love you," "When I loved you," they intoned.

A high-pitched, "I am sorry!" suddenly sailed through the class like the screech of a panicked bird. A woman had detached herself from the cluster of parents in the back and now rapidly advanced. Just before she reached Zhu she abruptly changed direction and rushed out of the room. The students stared at the doorway through which the woman had vanished while the piercing, "I am sorry!" reverberated in the room.

At the back of the class, the other parents fidgeted and glanced self-consciously at Zhu and at their teenage children, as if the woman's sudden departure revealed for the first time the absurdity of their hawk-eyed presence in class.

Did I say something wrong? Zhu wondered and turned toward the board to hide his embarrassment. A poster detached from the wall and gently glided to the floor. A girl rushed up and placed the poster carefully on the desk. Maybe she felt ill, Zhu thought and a shower of yellow chalk rained on the floor when he used too much force in underlining the verbs.

"For next week you'll memorize the tenses," he called out and drew a thick circle around a list on the board. He wrote directly over the pale Chinese characters that lingered on the board from an earlier class.

"Study carefully because there will be a quiz," he instructed the students, surprising even himself with the announcement. He wiped his forehead with his hand. Maybe it had been too hot for the woman in the classroom, he thought and kept going.

When he sensed that time was almost up he glanced at the watch on his desk. Nearly four o'clock, he saw with relief.

"Students, rise! I will see you next week!"

"Thank you, *Laoshi*," the students called out, but even before their voices had rippled to the front Zhu had already stepped into the hallway's shadowy silence. He quickly walked to the small, windowless room where he and the other tutors stored their coats and bags. If I get out quickly, he thought, I can clear my head by walking instead of taking the bus and still get to my shift in time.

Just then a girl stepped into the room.

"I am very sorry to disturb you, *Laoshi*, but my mother is outside," the girl said while staring at the floor.

She wore a black sleeveless t-shirt with rhinestone lettering over a long white cotton dress. Her legs were covered in rolled up jeans, and her long shiny hair concealed part of a pretty face. To avoid looking at her, Zhu rummaged in his canvas bag. Not another parent, Zhu thought. I gotta get out of here.

"My name is Sandy and I am in your class," she added when Zhu did not respond, using her English name that she had adopted in keeping with the rules of *English First!* There was a moment of silence that seemed to fill the space between them, as if more air had been pumped in. Extra tutoring, Zhu thought, another parent who wants to hire me on the side to pay a little less. He wanted to leave but also knew that these side deals, though against the rules at *English First!*, were an easy way to make extra money.

"I need to go," he mumbled but did not move.

The woman who had rushed from Zhu's classroom earlier now burst into the room. As soon as she spotted Zhu she caught herself and stood still, suddenly composed and with an expectant expression as if *he* had requested the meeting.

"*Laoshi*, I was so moved by the story you distributed today," she exclaimed while the girl shrank against the doorframe. No "hello," no apology, no awareness that not everybody might be part of her script. Without turning her head the woman pressed her elegant purse into the girl's hands and, elbows by her side and palms together, faced Zhu.

"You are an inspired and exemplary young man for writing a story as moving as the story of Chang'e," the woman said and looked directly at Zhu. Although she was surely twice his age, her eyes were radiant and her face seemed to absorb all of the light in the dank office. Zhu dropped his hands by his side.

"It was only a grammar exercise," he responded awkwardly and looked at the doorway. What is this about? he thought and reached for his bag. Chang'e? The lady who got separated from her husband and ended up a fairy on the moon? If this woman here wants to hire me as a tutor for her daughter she can just say it and I don't need to stay, he thought, but waited nonetheless.

When there was no response he looked up. Tears glistened on the woman's face.

He let go off his bag and handed the woman a rough paper napkin from a stack sitting on top of the scratched metal desk. The woman dabbed at her cheeks.

"Mom, let's go," the girl suddenly burst out, as if trying to break from her role of being an extra in this scene.

But something in the woman's way of talking had caught Zhu off guard. He knew the story of Chang'e, and even if there was no connection between it and his class he had always liked the tale. A woman out of reach on the moon but never forgotten by her grieving husband, he remembered his mother explaining to him when the moon had hung like a ripe melon above their town on summer nights.

He glanced at the woman's face and saw that her tears were now dabbed away. Gorgeous, he thought to his astonishment. He quickly looked away but also did not want to look at the student in the doorway, with that indignant teenage pout so familiar from all of his classes. She is absolutely beautiful, he thought and felt himself getting excited, wondering, why have I never noticed her?

And then, not knowing what to say or do, with two quick steps he squeezed past the two women and slipped out of the door.

* * *

Later that Saturday, Zhu sat at the counter at Fang's Café to start his shift. The amber-colored dusk had settled quickly on this quiet part of Shanghai, a few blocks east of the neon splendors of Huaihai Lu. Zhu had lit a cigarette and watched the handful of customers slouched in their velvet chairs, chewing peanuts while sipping tea or beer. He had placed his sketchbook next to the register and with an expensive pen that he had shoplifted at an art store near the Academy he meticulously inked the scene of the woman rushing from the classroom.

With only an occasional interruption from ringing up checks and preparing drinks, Zhu carefully sketched a female figure striding briskly to the left, a flowing scarf pressed over her mouth and the other hand clutching her chest. She is fleeing something, he thought while sketching versions that became increasingly abstract. Remote like Chang'e, it flashed through his mind while on the page appeared the silhouette of a half-turned woman centered on a single glistening tear. For a few minutes, Zhu filled the rest of the page with a tight grid of short, black strokes. The figure now stood out against that darkness as a ghost buffeted by a fierce storm.

Zhu pinched a pin from a tray next to the register and pierced a hole in the paper where he had marked the woman's single tear. While his colleagues reached around him for cups, glasses, saucers, and bottles of beer, Zhu held up the notebook with the page apart from the spine and squinted his eyes. He carefully enlarged the hole.

"Cool picture," a fellow waiter said. "Is that the Lady in the Moon?"

"Nah," Zhu responded. "It's just someone I saw today." He carefully slipped the page inside his sketchbook.

At the end of his shift, Zhu counted the cash from the register and put the coins back in the drawer. He slipped rubber-banded wads of bills into a white canvas bag, hid that bag at the bottom of a freezer under cartons of frozen food, and shut the lights. He keyed in a code for the alarm system, slung his bag over his shoulder, locked the doors, and slowly rode his bike home. In his apartment, he stripped to his underwear, poured some Chivas Regal from a bottle he'd bought off one of the other waiters, and sat on the bed. He taped the picture over the frosted pane in his room's door and covered the rest of the small window with packing paper. When he closed the curtains to shut out the neighboring hotel's neon lights, through the pinpricked tear the faintest ray of light shone from the hallway into the dark room. Zhu cupped his hand around the hole, put his mouth over his hand's opening, and closed his eyes. For a few moments, while his face was completely still, he thought he could take in breaths of light streaming through his cupped hand. Abruptly, he let himself fall backward on the bed, and thinking of the woman who had fled from his class slid his hands down his belly and under the elastic of his briefs.

* * *

Since coming to Shanghai, Zhu had developed certain habits that he did not intend to break.

Sex every time a girl slept over, regardless of how tired or drunk they both were when reaching his place.

"What's the point otherwise," Zhu had explained to a fellow student who was astonished upon hearing about his late night activities. "Why take someone home if it's not gonna get you off?"

Never breakfast at home, only minimal conversation after getting up, and ten minutes tops to get out of the door in the morning.

"I gotta work on my films," Zhu uttered not as an apology but because he knew that his film studies were a magnet for the girls he met.

"He's super cool," the girls explained afterwards, "and he doesn't have a lot of free time," when their friends asked them why he rarely called them back.

There were more unspoken rules: nothing to be placed on a small table by the door, even if every other surface was littered with objects and clothes. Wordlessly he'd lift a girl's cell phone or purse from the table and place it on the floor, or on top of a pile of clothing on the couch or on the TV set. Like his heart, the little table was to stay untouched and bare. And no terms of endearment, no matter how many times a girl slept over, and never any mention of her to his parents, even if she noisily prepared dinner in the tiny kitchen while he chatted with Mom and Dad on the phone a few feet away.

There was no point in trying to convince Zhu to

throw the moving boxes out of the kitchen, or to ask him to drop a shift at work or cancel on his friends so the girl in question could spend time with him alone. A nice dinner, a stroll along quiet streets, a nightcap at another restaurant, hard and unforgiving sex followed by some cuddling, but then heart-breaking silence on his part for days at a time.

The girls who hoped for more tried in vain to ward off his charms. But they all drowned in his brown eyes, deep like Tibetan lakes. There they stayed, immobile and defenseless, like insects trapped in amber. And while sitting at the counter at Fang's Café, Zhu resurrected these girls, one by one, on the pages of his notebook, as gingerly as an entomologist sticking pins through the shells of gossamer-winged insects for a museum case. With his fine-tipped pen, Zhu interlaced jots, lines and marks to remember these girls' features as if through a microscope. He labored over these diaphanous drawings for days, even if he had met the girl only for one night. This is where Zhu was truly in love, with his pen and in his memory. With his pen he squandered on these women the love and attention they so hopelessly sought from him.

* * *

"A parent wants to meet with you about the English course," the secretary from *English First!* said when Zhu answered his phone while seated in a barbershop.

It was the Tuesday after the woman's rushed departure from his classroom, and while Zhu talked, the young barber with a spiky hairdo held the buzzing razor inches from his neck.

"I can't talk right now," Zhu said.

"She said it's urgent," the secretary retorted.

"I'll stop by in a little while," Zhu said and ended the call.

I've never had a parent complain, he thought while letting the barber finish. Maybe it's about another tutoring job, but then the parent wouldn't call the Institute directly.

A half an hour later he walked into the Institute's office in a non-descript white tiled building near Zhongshan Park. His neckline was a hint paler where hair had covered the skin during the past week.

"What did she say?" Zhu asked by way of greeting. He was worried that a parent's complaint could lose him the lucrative teaching gig.

"I could not figure out what she wants," the young secretary responded. "She refused to say what this was about and only said it's urgent."

"I hope it'll be okay," Zhu replied without conviction.

"Oh, I'm sure you'll be fine," the young woman added quickly. She moved her computer screen to catch Zhu's gaze.

"But she said that she has to meet you before the next class," the young woman said with an air of importance and added conspiratorially, "I haven't told the director anything." Zhu glanced at the door next to her desk.

"Oh, he hasn't been here in weeks," the secretary assured Zhu. "He just calls from his car and tells me what to do. But don't worry, I didn't say a word to him."

"So what else did this parent say?" Zhu asked.

"She wants to meet you privately. She gave me the name of a restaurant on Xiangyang Lu near Fuxing Lu. It's called something like Café Blue. I wrote it down." She handed him the paper.

"Her name is Shi Weisha, and her daughter is in your 2:30 class on Saturdays. Do you want me to do anything?" she said eagerly, hoping for an opportunity to help.

Instead of responding Zhu picked up his bag and put in his earphones.

"Let me know what happens," the woman called out but Zhu could no longer hear her cheerful, "take good care!"

* * *

Make a good impression, Zhu thought and put on a grey striped vest over his only white shirt two days later. Maybe it won't be so bad, he thought, and brushed back his long hair with his hand. Then he set off for Café Blue. He pushed through a crowd in front of an electronics market and tried to determine the entrance for the brand-new café next door. Finally, he stepped into a gallery filled with fake antiques and was shown by a salesgirl how to access the café's serving area through an unfinished doorway. Near the windows a woman sat with hands folded in her lap. Her fitted, double-buttoned brown linen dress was sharply creased and cinched with an elegant belt. She wore high-heeled brown pumps and had crossed her feet at the ankles under her chair.

No bag, no phone, no sunglasses on the table in front of her. The woman seemed utterly unencumbered. She turned toward Zhu with a face full of expectation, as if she was about to embark on a journey. Zhu recognized her instantly as the mother who had run out of his classroom a week before. He also knew as soon as he sat down in front of this alert, composed and gorgeous woman that this time it was he who was about to drown.

"I am sorry I am late," Zhu said upon sitting down. The woman did not respond but gazed at Zhu intently with her dark eyes. Then she started speaking as if resuming a conversation that had simply stopped for a moment while Zhu took his seat.

"I married my husband when I was very young, and my daughter will have two parents until college. There's no question of divorce for people like us; our families wouldn't stand for it. We want our daughter to attend university in the UK where my husband went to school. The arrangement is fine, and none of this should be of any concern for you."

She took a small sip of tea, as if her remarks and their meeting in this café were perfectly self-evident.

"I have been observing your classes for my daughter for the past year. And last week, when you read the exercise with the verbs, I knew that you had written just for me *'I love I loved I loved'*."

She said the last words in English, making an effort to pronounce them correctly. It was the only moment when she seemed unsure of herself.

Zhu kept looking down at the table to avoid her face. The pale brown linen dress appeared to him like the exquisite binding of a rare book. He picked up a napkin and folded it into a small square.

"It was just a grammar exercise," he began without

looking up but then stopped speaking, sensing her eyes were on him. Zhu recrossed his legs and extended them fully, shifting again in his seat to find space next to the small café table. The woman did not move and now his calves were only inches from hers. Zhu stopped shifting his position. Leaving her legs very close to his but not touching him, she signaled a waitress for more tea.

"I love your teaching," she said while the waitress placed another setting in front of Zhu. "You have every reason to be proud of it. It's wasted on the kids in your class, including my daughter," she continued. "But it's changed my life to be there every Saturday."

"Oh, it's just a language class," Zhu said to dismiss the compliment but found it hard to take his eyes off her face. And then, within the span of several seconds, he convinced himself utterly, completely that he had indeed carefully composed the grammar exercise only for this gorgeous woman sitting before him now.

I must have noticed her before that day in class, he thought but couldn't get it fully straight in his mind.

"You are very kind to praise my teaching," Zhu tried to fend her off one last time. But this was just a formality now. He reached for some peanuts in an effort to tear his eyes off her. He had the sensation of not looking at the woman across the table in a bustling café but through a pinhole as in the drawing taped to his door. And just as his pen had shrouded the page on that sketch the woman in her brown linen dress began to blot out the rest of Zhu's life.

He ordered a coke. She told him her name, Shi Weisha, which he had heard already from the secretary but now it sounded like a song. She talked about her daughter and her life while they ate peanuts and almond cookies, drank tea, and smoked. Although it was late afternoon Zhu felt as if the sun was just coming up. When he shifted in his seat the denim of his jeans accidentally grazed Weisha's calves. They both stopped moving instantly and gently turned the accidental touch into intention. For the following few minutes, both of them kept their legs still. Zhu glanced up from underneath his long bangs and caught Weisha's eyes. She held his gaze and they both knew that they knew.

"*Laoshi*, thank you for your time," Weisha said formally before they parted. "I will be sure not to miss Saturday's class." She disappeared in the crowd.

* * *

The following Saturday Zhu was nervous before class. Get there just before class begins, he thought. Don't be crazy! He admonished himself. A parent in your class! You'll get into all sorts of trouble! He managed to arrive the minute class was scheduled to begin and did not glance at the parents huddled in the back. He got through class without a hitch and at four o'clock dismissed the students. He walked down the stairs with his headphones in his ears, trying not to let the disappointment get the better of him. In front of the building Weisha stood next to the stained concrete lions guarding the doors. A jolly market had sprung up where parents bargained for tutoring lessons for their offspring. Since Institute teachers were forbidden from tutoring students from their courses, these negotiations occurred quietly and quickly, off to the side.

"Would you like to go for a walk?" Weisha asked

Zhu by way of greeting.

So I wasn't imagining this, Zhu thought. The two of them peeled off from the crowd like another parent and teacher about to strike a quick and furtive deal. Maybe she's interested, he thought and felt sweat forming on his palms.

They wandered the tree-lined streets near the school. Zhu felt light-headed and accidentally bumped into Weisha's side several times, as if his footing were not steady. He had not looked at her face.

"Would you like to get some tea or a snack?" Zhu asked when they circled back on Fenyang Lu for the second or third time.

Weisha did not respond immediately.

Zhu added while they continued walking, "I am willing to do anything, in fact."

Weisha sought out his face, took out her phone and signaled for him to wait. Zhu stood on the sidewalk while she advanced several steps. There is really something going on here, he thought.

After a few words out of Zhu's earshot, Weisha snapped her phone shut and hailed a cab. She quickly climbed into the gold-colored car and ignored another woman who rushed toward the cab with cries of protest. More in an effort to escape the embarrassing scene than to steal the cab, Zhu slipped in. The driver flinched when the young woman slammed her bag on the car while he pulled into traffic. Inside, Weisha leaned against the seat and closed her eyes. She's probably going to find a restaurant a bit more out of the way, Zhu thought, and could not think of anything to say.

A few minutes later the taxi pulled into a driveway

underneath a Motel 168 next to the elevated highway. Before Zhu could reach his wallet Weisha had paid the driver. They got out and Weisha walked ahead of Zhu through the glass doors into the low-ceilinged lobby. While she handed the receptionist her identity card and filled out the papers, Zhu leaned against a nearby wall and stared at the floor.

Weisha turned around and, with a key card in her hand, walked toward Zhu and the elevators. Even before the elevator door had fully closed behind them Zhu wrapped his denim-clad leg around Weisha's hip and placed his hands around her neck. By now the doors had closed, and with one hand he gently stroked her back, and with the other tentatively pushed up her skirt a bit. His eyes were closed and he could smell her hair, which reminded him of freshly cut wood. When they walked into the cramped room on the 15th floor, the small white television set in the room showed a group of young actors extolling the virtues of a product for tinting grey hair. For the next few hours, while the television droned on and without turning off the bright neon overhead light, Zhu and Weisha made love.

*   *   *

The next evening, Weisha sent Zhu a text message to meet at the Xintiandi shopping arcades in a German-themed restaurant. They ordered tall glasses of wheat beer in which floated round lemon slices that looked like setting suns.

"My husband left earlier than planned for Chengde. He moved to Beijing for business a year ago and usually comes home only for the weekends, but I stayed in Shanghai so that Dao Ming can finish school. Dao Ming is at an auntie's house tonight to watch a talent show on TV. She knows that we do not intend to live together after she finishes high school."

Weisha took a cigarette from the pack lying on the table and waited for Zhu to light it for her.

"I've told her that I've asked you to tutor me to prepare for a business trip later this summer. I'm not sure if she even heard me, but if anybody sees us we can just switch to English and we're fine." Weisha laughed and added, "I think you should teach me some English, in fact. I might need it when I have to support myself. Why don't we start at Motel 168 tonight."

Zhu looked at her, cautiously, trying to gauge whether or not she was serious.

She smiled at him and laughed again.

"*It's okay*," she said in English. "You're not going to get in trouble – I work with a lot of foreign clients and need to keep my English up."

Zhu signaled the waitress for the check. He could hardly believe it. She wanted to go back to the hotel! He placed a bill on the table and rose so quickly that he almost spilled the two beers they had barely touched.

When they left the mall a driver from a pack of cabbies hurried to his idling car and took them to the hotel. Weisha approached the desk with cheerful indifference to the staff's possible opinions about the nature of her and Zhu's brief stays. When she presented her identity and credit cards the young receptionist took them with one hand, and then smiled with embarrassment at having dropped her manners. She deferentially returned with both hands Weisha's cards, the proper way.

"Thank you, Ms. Shi," she said while Zhu waited on a white couch under an artificial tree studded with white plastic orchids. Before the elevator doors had closed Weisha had slipped her cool hand around his neck, and his knees grew weak.

After an hour or so Weisha checked her phone. She kissed Zhu on his eyebrows and got up. Through the wall-sized window that separated the bedroom from the small bathroom Zhu watched Weisha take a shower. She had not turned on the light and quickly rinsed off. With her long hair pinned up she looked even more beautiful to Zhu. He watched her from the bed, his head turned toward the side and his eyes heavy with fatigue. She stepped from the shower and toweled off, now almost invisible through the fogged-up window. Then Weisha leaned forward and rested briefly against the glass, leaving a brief imprint of her mouth, hands, and breasts before returning to the room.

Zhu quickly pulled on underwear, jeans and a shirt, while Weisha applied lipstick, fixed her hair with a metal clip, and put her phone in her purse.

"Let's go, sleepy," she said and with a kiss on Zhu's lips opened the door.

Downstairs the same clerk still worked the desk. She cheerfully greeted Weisha with "Hello, Ms. Shi," and pulled the reservation from a folder. Weisha paid for the room, walked out of the lobby doors, and hailed a cab. Zhu felt weightless, happy, and a bit drunk.

"I love you," he mouthed into the empty street while watching the cab drive off. "I love you, sweetheart," he said, astonished at his own words.

*　*　*

When his head rested on her neck during their brief visits to Hotel 168, and also when he entered her, Zhu forgot himself and yet felt totally there. It was not the sex, or not the sex alone, that made him content. It was the strangely timeless hours spent in the motel's small, green-on-green rooms where they played and lounged atop the sheets, sipped water from small bottles or drank cheap wine out of paper cups, laughed, played more, made love, napped, cuddled and talked. And it was the few hours they occasionally sat in his cramped apartment that made Zhu content and forget his rules. He had finally cleared out the kitchen, scrubbed the bathroom and fixed the torn curtains. Weisha's keys, phone and purse cluttered the side table in the hall, and Zhu did not like to look at the table's bare surface after she left.

Weisha was the ocean for Zhu, and after each meeting he was swept out further into sea. His hands were everywhere on her, and he sometimes held her so tight as to keep from drowning. To him she was both life raft and roiling sea. There were moments when the waters were calm, nothing stirred, and all they did was breathe. Weisha gently placed her lips near Zhu's open mouth while he lay on his back, and for long minutes they inhaled and exhaled, their lips touching ever so slightly to allow air to escape on the side. Zhu hoped that in this mock resuscitation his longing for her could be stilled. Instead he left each of their encounters hungry for more.

* * *

Now it was mid-winter and Zhu had yet to come up for air. He had tried several times, gasping and rushing up with flailing legs and arms to disentangle himself from this woman's love. He had deleted Weisha's number from his phone and then reprogrammed it as many times when she called next. He had forced himself to go out with girls his age, but then taken them home and into his bed with Weisha on his mind. One night after he'd sent a girl home, explaining that he had to work, he tore all of the pages from his sketchbook on which he had drawn the characters of Weisha's name in many variations. But later he crammed the torn-out pages into a drawer instead of the garbage bin. He picked fights with Weisha and sobbed with clenched teeth and trembling shoulders when she forgave him, and then he cried again when she held him in his arms after they made love. He had tried to reach the bottom of his feelings by forcing Weisha into dramatic fights and scenes. None of this had worked to push himself out of her love.

When he pulled shifts at Fang's Café or stared at the monitors in the computer lab at school, Zhu willed himself to switch his phone off or leave it in his bag. He tried to convince himself that he checked for messages only casually at the end of the day, as if it were an afterthought rather than something he'd been itching to do for hours. His lips tightened slightly each time his phone birthed the tiny star that signaled a new message, and he punched the keys rapidly, as if to make up for lost time, to see who had placed the call.

Weisha never inquired about Zhu's week, his friends, or his plans for when she was not around.

"I'm not going to be able to see you until Monday,"

she said to him in the elevator after a few hours in the Motel 168, very early on a Friday morning. Before Zhu could express his disappointment, she continued. "I want you to have a great weekend!"

She stepped from the elevator into the lobby, and Zhu was not sure whether she planned on having a great weekend without him, or whether she wanted him to have fun.

"I wish I could see you before Monday," Zhu tried meekly.

"Yes of course," Weisha responded as if the previous sentence hadn't been spoken, "I'd love to see you before Monday. What's good for you?"

Zhu was defeated again. The night before they had discussed the animated short film he had to finish by Monday, and how important this assignment was for him. They both knew he had no time.

"Actually, it won't really work for me," Zhu said, feeling tricked into saying no, although he couldn't quite determine how.

They stepped out of the glass foyer into the hotel's driveway.

"What do you think the front desk people think of us?" Zhu asked.

"They worry about their own lives," Weisha responded and kissed him in full view of the sleepy cabbies waiting for a fare. Together they rode through Shanghai in the morning haze, drowsy from sex and lack of sleep.

After he had dropped off Weisha, Zhu redirected the driver to the Film Academy. He worked through the weekend, letting whole worlds arise on the monitor in front of him. He had placed his phone next to the screen, and listened to the songs he and Weisha had played at the hotel.

On Monday morning very early, he met Weisha for only an hour at the 168 Motel.

"You need to sleep to be ready for your presentation," she had said when he called but at the hotel stopped neither Zhu's hands nor lips.

"What I need to do is be with you," Zhu had responded and lifted her on top of him, breathing in her hair. Later, when Weisha had fallen asleep, Zhu listened to the morning traffic build to its rush hour crescendo. In his head he drew images of the two of them holding each other, with their clothes pooled around their feet. They looked like statues rising out of stone and Weisha's hair poured down, in his imagination, to far below her knees.

An hour later Zhu waited in a classroom to present his work to CCTV representatives on a scouting visit to his school. "I Am In Control," it said on the screen above him while the suits filed in and his teachers nervously sat on chairs along the wall. Zhu quickly checked his phone for a message from Weisha. The officials extended their cards and Zhu reciprocated by handing them his self-designed acetate name cards.

A group of students crowded in the hallway outside of the glass-walled presentation room until a teacher flipped the blinds to block their view. With his phone placed on the table next to the computer, Zhu seemed all but indifferent to his fellow students' excitement and to the officials' authority. After the presentation a high-ranking member of the delegation turned to Zhu's teacher. "He seems ready to take on bigger projects, and we want to talk to the Director about his future placement."

The teacher's tense face brightened. He quickly ushered the officials out of the door and shooed away the students crowding in the hallway. When the delegation walked down the hall, Zhu's classmates cut a respectful berth around them.

"We need men like you to add Chinese-language cartoons to compete with foreign programming on our airwaves," the official said and Zhu's teacher nodded in agreement.

"Zhu is our top student this year and will go far," the teacher said.

"I am in control," Zhu quietly read off the cover page of his printed presentation that he now handed the officials. He glanced at his phone and saw that there was no message. Why hadn't she called? he thought. She knew the presentation would be over by now. He closed his eyes for a moment and then shut down the computer.

While the officials chatted quietly off to one side of the room, the drawing teacher turned to Zhu.

"Chinese television wants to compete," he said. "You don't look happy, but you should! Forget about footage from the party congress and reports on fisheries set up in the Red Sea. They know that all the kids download foreign films instead of watching their programs. They'll give you control over your show. They loved the proposal. If they commission you to design a show for CCTV, your career is set."

Zhu checked his phone again and when there was no message, his stomach clenched. He turned his face away from his teacher's expectant gaze.

"*Laoshi*, I have to go," he said and walked off,

giving the impression that he was so confident and so absorbed in his work that he did not even have time to chat.

I Am In Control, it said on Zhu's notebook in artfully inked, old-fashioned characters. But when he was with Weisha he felt not only that he wasn't in control, but that he did not want to be. He did not know what to do when he was with her: he wanted to talk, walk around, sit and gaze into her eyes in silence, make love, get into a taxi, get drunk, touch her hands, hold her breasts, walk slowly down quiet streets, look at her, kiss her, have a long meal.

"This is something she likes," Zhu told himself while letting go of her hand to gently stroke her hair, and then reaching for her hand again a second later. He had accidentally pulled a barrette out of her hair and Weisha laughed. She deftly piled her hair back on top of her head. Then she took both of Zhu's hands, held them between her palms, and kissed him softly on his eyelids.

*   *   *

On a Monday morning at Fang's Café, Zhu served jasmine tea and lemon juice to a flushed-looking woman with a shiny ponytail. She and a friend, a woman Zhu knew slightly, were the only customers. Just as Zhu passed their table he overheard the woman with the ponytail.

"He has a lady friend," she hissed at his friend and Zhu felt a shiver run over his shoulders.

This business with Weisha is going get me into trouble, he thought, but then he dismissed the thought.

Let them talk. He casually pushed the sleeve of his black shirt up above his tattoo. He traced the pattern with his fingers while walking with the tray under his arm back to the counter. It's going to be me who shapes my life, he thought. But by the time he had reached the counter Zhu nearly clutched his upper arm where the characters for Weisha were inked under his skin. Weisha, he thought, is she going to call today? He stood still for a moment, tightening his fingers' grip on his tattoos until it began to hurt and another waiter gently edged him aside to reach the counter.

Like an addict Zhu wanted Weisha's time and attention especially when he knew that it was he who kept himself from having more.

"I want to see you tonight," he said on Sunday morning when she finally picked up the phone.

Weisha responded instantly, "I do too, what time works for you?"

Nothing came of it. That night Zhu and a fellow student were scheduled for a coveted time slot in the Academy's computer lab. Zhu texted message after message into his silent phone only to erase each missive before pushing *send*.

"I want to go away with you," Zhu finally sent a text. Instantly, Weisha turned everything into his responsibility.

"Where to I'm ready," came the response as if she, the wealthy, married older woman with a teenage daughter in his class and lots to lose, were truly free.

* * *

"It's quite an attractive way to pay for your study

fees," his fellow waiters joked after Weisha met Zhu one evening following his shift at Fang's Café. "Has she taught you a few tricks?" they teased.

"It's the way for handsome guys like you to make money in the New China," they continued laughingly. When they saw Zhu's pained face they stopped their jokes.

"How are you doing?" they asked days later with real concern when Zhu walked with his self-designed bag slung low over his shoulder and his eyes heavy from lack of sleep. "You gotta take care of yourself," they said. "She's great and all, but you can't let a married woman ruin your life!"

As much as Zhu wanted to regain his freedom, he also did not want to end things with Weisha. He had grown equally attached to the sense of nervous anticipation and unrequited longing and to the pleasures of actually seeing her. During the week, the tide of Zhu's day turned the moment Weisha's name appeared on his phone's tiny screen. Until he received a signal, he felt parched and panicked like a fish cast ashore wriggling to reach the sea. Yet during those anxious spells between Weisha's calls and their meetings Zhu also felt desperately and wretchedly alive. He covered pages of his notebook with sketches and drawings, and dispensed with his daily tasks as swiftly as a jet slicing through low-hanging clouds. Everything but Weisha had become secondary and erstwhile challenges now seemed trivial; nothing but Weisha's actions had substance or weight. He passed through the world with the slightly aloof air reserved for those who are hopelessly in love.

When they finally met, after flurries of text

messages to lock in one hour or so, he barely calmed down sufficiently to enjoy the moment. On a gloomy January afternoon they lay naked on the motel bed and Weisha's face was turned toward him, with her eyes closed. It was restful in the room, and the slanted blinds cast a grid of soft gray stripes on the sheets. Zhu feared that their time together would be up soon and quickly checked the time. Weisha had opened her eyes and saw him glancing at his watch. She closed them again but her jaw was more set now, in what appeared to Zhu tensed in the suspicion that he had not fully relaxed in her arms. A shadow passed over her face and Zhu, not knowing whether he felt better with her near or far, buried his head on her chest.

"All week," Weisha said after stepping across a gash in the sidewalk where workers laid electric cable, "I think of little else but your eyes like Tibetan lakes. While I work I recall the sound of your voice reciting English words. When I go to sleep I think of you inside of me."

She ignored the dust-covered laborers who rested on their shovels to stare open-mouthed at the elegant woman holding a young hipster's hand. In her slim skirt, matching jacket and high heels she passed through a gap in the temporary fencing set up around the worksite. While avoiding the workers' eyes, Zhu followed her self-consciously, his artfully torn black jeans, untucked shirt and shaggy hair eliciting stares of disapproval.

At the Motel 168 a little while later, Weisha traced the outline of Zhu's tattoo up his arm. Close to his shoulders the complicated pattern was crowned by a subtle variation on two Chinese characters.

"Wei-sha," she said, surprised. "You put my name on your arm. Weisha."

She smiled indulgently, aware of the power she had over him. Zhu nodded and wrapped his tattooed arm around her.

* * *

It had been almost a full year since Weisha ran out of Zhu's classroom with tears in her eyes. Since then, Zhu had lost control of every aspect of his life that had once mattered. Weisha's name was inked into his arm, onto the pages of his sketchbooks and echoed through his dreams. He knew he had to break free.

"I won't be able to come to class today," Weisha had texted in the morning.

"Damn!" he had yelled and punched his hand hard against the wall.

He had just put on a shirt and the vest he'd worn for their first meeting and was looking forward to the moment after class where they would be alone together. He briefly considered canceling class but there was not enough time to let his students know.

A thought arose in his head, unexpected and wildly welcome, like an empty cab in a downpour during rush hour on Nanjing Lu.

* * *

A few hours later Zhu stood as on every Saturday between the gaudy posters of European castles, scenic villages, and waterfalls. Zhu made an effort not to think of his phone in his front pocket with Weisha's text messing up his plans. He was focused on one thing only now.

At the end of class, instead of leaving, Zhu rummaged through the desk. His hair hung down his forehead and he didn't brush it from his eyes even when a parent waited for a minute to ask a question. Then suddenly, as if responding to a cue, Zhu grabbed his bag and rushed to catch up with the last students exiting the door.

"Can I ask you to stay a moment," he mumbled to a girl just about to leave the room. "You're a good student, and perhaps you would like to work as an assistant for the lower grades next year."

The girl stared at the floor while Zhu made his case. A few minutes later they walked out of the building, past the two stained lions flanking the stairs and through the students and parents milling about. Zhu did not slow down and the girl had to hurry to keep up with him.

Some thirty minutes later, Zhu was panting heavily while the girl rocked astride him wearing nothing but her bra, her head bent back and her hands clutching his bare shoulders. His hand gripped her waist on the hard bed with lime-green sheets. Their clothes were scattered in heaps around the bed. Clumsily they changed positions and the girl yelped when she almost slid off the bed. Now Zhu was on top, breathlessly and exhaustingly trying to break free. The girl moaned, her eyes closed and her hands tightly around Zhu's back.

This time it had been Zhu who had walked up to the lobby desk and handed his residence card to the receptionist with both hands, the proper way. And it had not been Zhu but Weisha's teenage daughter, Dao

Ming, who had waited on the couch below the tree with the white plastic orchids while he had booked the room.

During the following week, Zhu and Dao Ming ate hotpot in a mall's food court packed with office workers, high school students, and young couples on a weeknight date. While the waitress placed small plates heaped with sliced vegetables on the table Zhu leaned across the steam to place his hand on the girl's cheek.

A few days later, Zhu and Dao Ming met at the Old China Reading Room near Fang's Café where Zhu's shift would start in an hour. They sat at one of the café's mismatched tables and sipped the kind of sweet tea that Zhu made at Fang's Café one block over. Sandy wore a long, thin scarf and matching finger-less gloves. Zhu had turned off his phone, and they chatted about her friends and the songs they liked, held hands, and otherwise behaved like any other young couple in search of love.

The following week it was back to English class. Zhu arrived in class at two o'clock sharp. The students had taken their seats, and this time Weisha was among the vigilant parents along the back wall. Zhu had written a sentence on the board and asked his students to deconstruct it by underlining it in colored chalk. For a moment the students paid equal attention to all parts, without skipping over pronouns or particles, nor instantly seizing on verbs to grasp the flow of life, or homing in on nouns as if existence were staked on substantives alone. In his students' notebooks different colors showed how every last one of these particles contributed to making up, finally, the whole word.

Zhu then returned to the exercise of reciting irregular

verbs from the beginning of the semester. And for the first time since that day in September when Weisha had detached from the back wall and catapulted into his life, he knew for a brief moment how time lost all meaning when anticipation, fulfillment and regret offered similar highs. In the back Weisha listened attentively. First silently and then in a soft whisper she mouthed the words that her teenage daughter and the other students called out to Zhu.

"Love, loves, loved," Weisha joined the class. From Zhu's position near the blackboard he could see daughter and mother in a single straight line. They both looked radiant. And they both thought exactly the same thoughts about him, even if at four o'clock sharp at the end of class, for one of them time with Zhu would end while for the other it would go on. While repeating for his captive audience of students, parents, lovers, "love, loved, loved," Zhu for a moment felt free. And he knew in his heart, with both mother and daughter drowning in his eyes that only Chinese, where *love, love, love* does not show distinction between past, present, and future, got it right.

SHANGHAI TAXI

They get in, they stay awhile, they get out. Sometimes they pay no attention at all to Gao, and at other times they talk his ear off, either telling him what he doesn't want to know or chattering into their phones without stopping to tell him where to go. One girl got in and explained to him, not that he'd asked, that the pants she was wearing were really her sister's, and that she had put them on so she could feel like her for a day "because she gets anybody she wants even though she's only a salesgirl in a record store." As if this made any sense: putting on someone else's pants to be that person, or getting just anybody. Gao remained silent and drove.

"But what I really want," the girl confided breathlessly while paying her fare as if letting him in on a secret, "was to keep my sister from going dancing. Her other pants were not dry yet. So tonight she'll stay home!" And with that triumphant statement she slammed the door and skipped toward a fast food stall in front of a hulking public sports center where she was greeted by a group of friends.

Gao listened and drove. He was focused on one thing only, and the passengers' chatter were just so much background noise, no different from the advertising jingle that rang out each time the meter was turned on. His hands tight on the steering wheel and his eyes glued to the road he tried to get across each intersection just as the lights had already turned red. He timed each approach just so that he could get to the line when the car in front of him had still crossed on green. Then he would jerk the cab forward and squeeze across on red before the traffic from the sides surged on.

It had started innocently enough, when Gao's girlfriend had responded to his questions about why she hadn't been able to see him for a few days, matter-of-factly, "I'm very busy right now preparing for exams."

Ever since that sentence Gao felt as if he was rushing to catch up. He had missed important cues, the other cabbies with whom he smoked and waited for his shift, explained to him afterwards. Important cues like the fact that Ling Ling had applied for a teacher's license in Beijing rather than Shanghai, and that she had not invited him out to eat with her parents when they had visited Shanghai the second time. Now he was trying to be ahead of things, first of all, but more importantly he was trying to store up extra time that the two of them could use when they got back together.

And he would get back together with Ling Ling! It was just a matter of time, or rather nothing but a matter of time. A matter of accumulating a few extra seconds and minutes that they could then use up jointly.

Gao squinted his eyes at a foreigner who waved with his palm toward him as if shooing him away. Wait – did the guy actually want the cab? Gao slowed down and the man hustled his two children toward the car. They climbed in and the man anxiously unfolded a large map of Shanghai in the back seat. Gao could neither see the map nor understand the man's broken

Chinese. Where did they want to go? Finally Gao heard one of the kids say, "Shanghai Zoo, Zoo."

"Across the whole city," Gao retorted but realized instantly that nobody in the back could understand. The kids sang along to the jingle that spelled out the cab company's name and telephone number when Gao flipped the meter up. Then they resorted to a language that he did not understand, and Gao focused on the traffic. Here was a rare chance! They approached an intersection under the elevated highway, and Gao saw on the digital ticker installed above the roadway that only a few seconds of green light were left. Two more cars ahead. One more car. He swerved quickly, cutting off a blue lorry and then sped his cab across the intersection just after the sign above his lane had counted down, *3, 2, 1, stop.*

Like the last beast behind a panicked herd the cab flew across the open space just before traffic roared in from left and right. In the backseat the man had flung his arm across the front of his children, pressing them tight into the seat.

Safely on the other side, Gao beamed at the easy victory. One light phase lasted at least three minutes! He slapped his steering wheel. When they had to wait on the ramp to the elevated highway he pulled a notepad from his breast pocket and jotted down "3 minutes" with a pen he took from the dashboard. Once he had added up enough of these fractions salvaged across blinking lights Gao would offer them to Ling Ling, after they would make up, as a gift.

* * *

Ling Ling had entered Gao's life through the backdoor of his cab.

"I am so sorry, *Shifu*!" the young woman had said at the end of her ride. She was frantically rifling through her bright blue purse, the pockets of her navy blue rain jacket, and then her purse again. "I think I forgot my wallet!"

Behind Gao cars started to honk and he had been forced to move. He had just flipped down the meter. 21 yuan, it read.

"This has never happened to me." Her face looked distraught and a bit frightened in the rear view mirror. "I don't know where my wallet is!"

He could not afford to cover her fare. Twenty-one kuai added up to two hours of pay, and there was no way his partner, the owner of the cab, was going to let him drive an additional two hours on his shift.

"You can use your bus pass to pay," Gao said and pointed at the sign next to the meter.

"I know," the woman responded. "But I don't have my wallet at all." She nervously craned her neck forward to look at him through the bubble of plexiglass that cocooned his seat.

"Is there any way I can give you the money later?" she asked, trying to catch his eye.

"I don't know," Gao said with a tone of defeat. "I work till 8."

Why had she gotten into his cab in the first place? If people had no money they shouldn't hail a cab. He wouldn't think of ordering a meal in a restaurant if he couldn't pay, so why did people think he would chauffeur them for free through Shanghai?

Once before Gao had called the dispatcher when a

couple had refused to pay because they claimed he had taken a longer route.

"Be careful who you pick up next time!" the voice on the other end of the phone had snapped and then hung up. The couple had looked at him smugly, as if they were in cahoots with the dispatcher, before exiting without paying the fare.

"Can you tell me where you will drop off the cab after your shift?" the woman now asked. Silently he handed her the company's card from a stack shoved under the radio console.

"I am really sorry," she repeated and, bunching the long tail of her blue raincoat in one hand so it wouldn't get stuck in the door, got out.

He sighed and slowed down for a woman in a slim skirt and matching jacket standing in the roadway.

"Motel 168, Jiangsu Road," she announced in a clipped voice through the open window before getting in. A young man with messy hair and sideburns shaped into narrow triangles quickly walked up to the cab and joined the woman in the back. Mother and son, Gao thought to himself and threaded his way back into traffic. He felt exhausted and frustrated at the traffic's slow pace. He had lost 21 kuai, and there was hardly any time to make up for it on this shift. When he glanced in the mirror he saw the woman brush the man's hair out of his forehead. Gao caught the man's gaze, full of excitement, which turned in that instant to self-consciousness. He quickly turned his eyes back on the traffic ahead.

At the Motel 168 Gao forced his cab through the endless stream of bicycles and mopeds that flowed out of the city like the garbage on the Huangpu River he had once watched after a heavy rainstorm being pulled out by the tide. He squeezed into the motel's narrow driveway, and took a commuter card from the woman's hand.

"Oh, let me pay," the young man hurried to say but the machine was already sputtering out the receipt. Gao noticed an intricate tattoo that climbed up the young man's left forearm, and how the pattern repeated like a faint shadow in a pen drawing on the bag he now pulled from the cab. Not quite mother and son, the thought flared up in Gao with disdain and a hint of envy, but rather one of those young guys who's found a better way of making money in the new China.

A delivery van, its dirty back doors half ajar and revealing tightly packed, elaborate floral arrangements, had stopped directly in front of his cab. He backed out of the driveway and slowly into traffic. It was dark now and Gao had to strain his eyes to look for fares. He hung a right, then another right, and then another one: one of his little tricks of forcing good luck his way. Three Western tourists got in with a Chinese. Giddy and loud, dressed in sharply creased clothes from the fake market, all bright colors and foreign labels, they asked Gao to turn on the radio.

He did as he was told, grateful to be roused from his gloomy mood by the good-natured group. They arrived at a little hotel near Fuxing Park. One of the tourists handed him 30 yuan and got out before he could return the change. That means I'm only 13 yuan short now, he thought happily while pulling away. Just on the next block he braked to a halt near a good-looking woman who took the front seat, her legs in black boots tightly pressed together and her hair in a shiny ponytail.

"Just a minute," she said while looking straight ahead and tapping a number into her cell phone. He flipped up the meter and idled the car until someone answered her call.

She named a street near the new train station that he did not know, and he mumbled an apology when he had to take out the map to find it. When they arrived the woman squinted her eyes at the dirty warehouses as if she expected someone to meet her.

"Wait a moment," she instructed him and made another call. What choice do I have? he thought gloomily since she did not leave the cab. His mood had lifted only for the few moments when the raucous four-some had filled his cab with laughter and the radio. They sat in silence in front of a steel-gated building for a good ten minutes, with the meter running. Gao wondered how it would be if he were the woman's driver, with nothing to do but to take her back and forth all day. But she looked anxious, somehow, in spite of her neat clothes and calm face, almost afraid, clutching her bag and with her back barely touching the seat, so straight was her posture. Gao sensed more than he knew that she was attractive, but he did not dare to glance at her from the side.

Another call, a different address. He drove and searched for the number of the alley she had indicated. He finally pulled into the narrow opening, careful not to scrape the cab's mirrors against the walls on either side. Another cabbie had gotten into an accident and they said he had to return home and borrow an enormous amount of money from his family and relatives to pay off the owner.

Slowly Gao threaded the car through the alley until

they reached the number they'd been searching for. He stopped the cab to idle the engine.

The woman pulled a book from her bag and started to read. Gao finally dared to glance at her and did so without moving his head. He was struck by her beauty, and by the gentle way she now flattened a page with her fingers. With a cheap pen she jotted a few characters in the book's margins.

A loud rapping on the cab's roof interrupted them. The woman very quickly shut the book, slipped it in her bag, opened the door and stepped out. Gao flicked down the meter and a heavy-set man shoved a bill through the open door. Gao leaned over to hand back the change but the pair had already walked off. He pulled the passenger door shut and watched in the rearview mirror while the two of them disappeared down the alley, the man with a rolling gait very close to the woman who walked, her back still noticeably straight, with her arms pressed closely to her sides. The silver bands on the heels of her boots flashed briefly as the pair passed through a perfectly round circle of light cast from a streetlight before disappearing from view.

Gao edged his way out of the alley down a dark road and with the next turn he ended up on a brightly lit ramp leading up to the new train station. He sighed in frustration when he saw dozens of other cabs ahead of him, inching toward the station. Then someone knocked on the window and quickly got in.

"You have to wait at the station's marked area," Gao protested meekly but after scanning the surroundings for a traffic guard, he flicked on the meter. Stone-faced, he pushed across four lanes of the glacially moving traffic, and then very slowly backed the cab down the emergency lane to the bottom of the ramp. The other cabbies, resigned to their wait, eyed him with envy.

Gao threaded his way through traffic to take the couple to a restaurant in the French Concession that was lit up with silk-covered lanterns swaying in the breeze. He was hungry, tired, and had to pee badly. He stopped the cab just off Dongping Road and sprinted past the statue of Pushkin into the public restroom where he nearly slipped and fell on a sopping wet floor. A man eyed him suspiciously and Gao hurried to get back to his cab, afraid he would get a ticket.

After he had relieved himself there was only little time left to return the cab on time, and Gao passed a man with a suitcase who flagged him down frantically.

At the car wash where he traded the car with his partner there was a small huddle of cabs, metallic blue, lime-green, silver, gold and magenta-hued Santanas all emitting their one-note Volkswagen hum like cattle sleeping on their feet, swaying slightly in the evening's soft glow. The drivers chatted idly while in line to gas up and get their cabs washed. They gossiped about which fare had taken them the farthest today, how long the wait at Pudong had been, how the new city surcharge was screwing them, and that the subway construction continued to be a bitch.

Ten minutes before eight, perfect timing, his partner could load his first fare at eight and continue with a full tank through the twelve-hour shift. Gao handed five yuan to a young guy to get his cab through the wash lane. He bought a few skewers of meat barbecued on a rain-pipe-cum-charcoal-grill from a guy who also sold cans of beer out of a cooler. With his back against a lamppost he kept an eye on his car while quickly chewing the tasty charred meat. Instantly he felt warmer, and exhaled with an open mouth to cool down the food and then, when the skewers were done, rested for a moment to relax.

Someone nudged him hard in the ribs.

"Hey," he said sharply and spun around angrily, having almost spilled his beer. The cabbie next to him gestured with his head and Gao saw a young woman a few feet away, very still amidst the idling cabs and the drivers squatting low or standing in small groups. The smoke from their cigarettes blended with the Santanas' exhaust, and amidst the haze, the metal and the men the woman looked forlorn. He quickly wiped his hand across his mouth when he realized that she was staring at him.

"Here is your 21 yuan," the woman said and stepped forward. She held four bills in her extended hands.

It took him a moment to understand.

"Do you remember?" she said, obviously in response to his blank expression. "I'm the woman who forgot her wallet this afternoon and I said that I would pay you tonight . . ."

"Of course, of course! Thank you!" He hadn't entertained the slightest hope that she would actually pay him. He took the money and stood there, embarrassed both at his lack of faith in her and because all of the other drivers now watched the two of them.

"Well, I guess I can go now," she said and began to turn, and then she said to nobody in particular, making sure they could all hear, "Can I get a taxi somewhere around here?"

Everybody within earshot burst into laughter. A

few drivers leapt to their feet and hustled to their cabs where they bowed theatrically, flung open doors, and shouted, "Lady, here's your ride," or "Take my cab! I got four stars for service!"

She wound her way through them as if she had just brought rain to a region that had suffered a drought for years. Gao did the one thing he'd been proud of ever since: He spoke up.

"I've just finished my shift so I cannot give you a ride," he said over the din, "But is there anywhere I can walk you?"

He gestured vaguely at the surroundings. The road was lined with grimy storefront shops where mechanics fixed carburetors and whole engines under glaring lights clamped to wire racks. A few dirty cars were parked at odd angles to the shops, like battle-weary soldiers waiting in a makeshift field hospital for triage. It was a perfectly safe neighborhood but Gao wanted to be courteous.

"There's a little restaurant here where the first crayfish have just arrived," he ventured, emboldened by the fact that she had slowed to listen.

"They fry the crayfish in rice wine, and they'll only be having them for a few days."

She looked at him quizzically. "You already ate dinner just now," she stated and gestured at the kebab sticks fanning out from his left hand.

"Oh, that's okay," he said and quickly dropped the sticks near some garbage on the sidewalk. She laughed again.

"Sure, I'd love to try the crayfish if you're still hungry" she said and walked ahead. "You have 21 yuan you can spend on me, that much I know!"

Catching up with her, he rubbed his eyes with one hand. He raised the other hand and almost smacked himself on the head, and hard, just to be sure. She had said yes! She had said *I'd love to try the crayfish!* He could feel the other drivers' stares in his back and almost hear their dirty jokes.

"Just a second," he remembered and yelled at the boy to hand the cab over to his partner.

A few minutes later Gao and the girl stepped over a torn-up sidewalk and then sat on plastic chairs in a small, neon-lit restaurant. The windows were postered with cut-out magazine pages showing women picking crayfish from gurgling country streams, and snapshots of crayfish staring beady-eyed into the camera next to beaming children with matching red vests and visors.

Several wooden crates with crayfish lined the wall underneath a blaring television set, and behind a plastic partition two sweaty cooks tossed a few crayfish at a time into large metal pans where the tiny lobsters danced on the hot metal before being doused with a hissing swig of wine.

"Quick! Quick! Pick-up!" the cooks yelled and slid plates on the shelf under a heating lamp.

Two waitresses rushed the plates to the tables. Gao and the girl, who had by now introduced herself as Ling Ling, sucked the meat from the spindly crayfish while watching a news program on the TV. He ordered a few beers and Ling Ling drank an orange soda. The crayfish had a light, tangy flavor that lingered with the hint of alcohol in which they had been cooked. Gao ordered sesame bread and for a while they did not talk.

The meal came out to exactly 22 yuan.

"See, it's a good thing I brought you the missing

fare today," Ling Ling joked when he paid, and handed him a single yuan coin. "Next time it'll be all on you!"

Gao broke into a smile and then looked away quickly, not wanting to show how happy this promise of another meal made him. They stepped over the concrete chunks that littered the torn-up sidewalk, and Gao lent Ling Ling his arm for support as if they had been a couple for a long time.

For a few months after that first meal, Gao and Ling Ling lived like that season's first batch of crayfish that had hissed and jumped on the stovetop of the tiny restaurant that night. They sizzled and danced along the city's sidewalks and only rarely came to rest anywhere for long, as if the ground were hot to the touch. They roamed through the tree-lined streets of the French Concession, and wandered for hours through the narrow canyons just off the Bund to emerge near the water and look across at the skyline of Pudong. When the weather turned warm they finally settled down in the manicured gardens of big new apartment complexes near artificial streams, playing Parcheesi on a plastic set that came in a little tin stamped with pictures of the Chinese Air Force. They ate in one-room restaurants along Wulumuqui Road that vibrated from the hulking air conditioning units, and where sullen waiters flung plates on plastic tablecloths nearly colorless from countless scrubbings. Or they watched the kids at the malls, making a sport of following teenagers who thought their shoplifting would go undetected.

"Nice socks you picked out there," Ling Ling would call out to a pair of girls descending on an escalator while they were going up, and then she laughed so hard at the girls' terrified faces that she had to sit on the floor on the next level until Gao had to help her get back up on her feet.

They spent nights and early mornings in an intoxicated rush that left both of them happily spent, and texted each other twenty, maybe thirty times each day. At the end of the summer, when the city sat humid and heavy like laundry that had been left in a machine overnight, they settled into a routine. In the mornings Ling Ling taught in her teacher-training program at a school near the airport in Hongqiao, and in the afternoons she worked in a travel agency wedged into a sliver of a store in a bleak mall to make money. Gao changed to mostly day shifts and met Ling Ling in the evenings so they could eat, walk home, and make love.

They did not talk about plans or about the future. Gao held back his questions and learned not to think ahead. He resisted the urge to find out her exact plans. You cannot force something to grow by pulling it higher, Gao thought to himself and waited for Ling Ling to tell him what would happen when she got a full-time teaching job. He could hardly believe his good fortune of having this beautiful girl all to himself and did not want to mess things up.

"Let things develop naturally," his cousin advised him on the phone when he called his hometown on the weekends. "City girls don't like to be pressured too much."

And as it were, things were going well. During Golden Week, Ling Ling's parents had mailed Gao a present of two cartons of cigarettes from their hometown and a special tea that would keep him awake while driving his shifts. Sometimes Gao would stop his cab in a side street, lean against the hood and deeply inhale the tobacco smoke to taste something from the place that had produced someone as beautiful as Ling Ling.

By Mid-Autumn Festival Gao had successfully lobbied the manager enough to work more day shifts, and only three nights a week. He drove passengers from the dusky apartment buildings of Puxi to the steep glass facades of Pudong and back, criss-crossing the city without going anywhere. From his rear-view mirror dangled a tiny bamboo good-luck charm in the shape of a lantern made by Ling Ling's mother, and Gao felt that this token would surely guide their love.

At night he delivered the cab to his partner and cashed out. When he opened the apartment door, his eyes fell on Ling Ling bathed in the TV's blueish glow, kneeling amidst shiny discs strewn about the floor like the petals of a flower from the future. She looked lost in reverie but then pulled Gao down playfully to kiss him when he squeezed past. She was choosing a DVD from among the dozens of films she had purchased during the summer. She searched for scenes, as she had explained to Gao, that "held the key to how we can change fate."

While Gao changed out of his driver's uniform Ling Ling fast-forwarded and rewound movies, skipping back and forth to find a particular scene. Gao settled on the bed and with drooping eyelids watched the films flicker soundlessly under Ling Ling's direction while the radio played Taiwanese pop. Ling Ling's favorite films were the inspirational kind with casts of athletes or dancers who sported good looks but could rarely act. She slipped a shiny disc into the DVD player and on came *Perfect* with John Travolta, a star that Gao recognized from bootlegged copies of *Grease* he had watched with his baby sister long ago at home. Ling Ling skipped forward to the workout sessions.

"This is where we learn that he's not been honest," she explained while Gao sat up on the bed to get a full view of the screen. The actors' moves looked strained and jerky over the sound of the radio playing softly by his bedside.

"Wait," Ling Ling said as if Gao were about to leave, which he had no intention of doing. She stopped the film and rifled through the DVDs.

"Here, look at this one," she said while switching discs.

"It's exactly the opposite," she said and clicked through the film with the remote.

Gao looked sleepily at Ling Ling's back, her hair cascading from a loosely pinned-up ponytail, and tried to pay attention. He was happy on the bed with her only a few feet away comfortably on the floor. He made an effort not to doze off.

"In this movie we learn that if a man wants to be honest but has no courage, the woman suffers" she explained.

He had no plans of making her suffer. I am honest, he thought, and I may lack courage but I have nothing to hide. He valiantly tried to understand the scene.

"Look, there!" Ling Ling said and gestured at the screen. A famous American actor whose face grimaced down daily on Gao's cab from the side of a towering mall on Nanjing Lu had just stepped off a train. The actor watched a curvy dancer through the windows of a studio. Ling Ling had asked Gao to watch the scene before but he failed to see its significance. Still there was something he could contribute.

"That's when he has to decide whether to go into the studio, or continue home to his family," he said.

Ling Ling was delighted.

"Exactly!" she confirmed his response while tracking the man's movement across the screen with one finger. "It's a test of courage!"

Gao settled back down, pleased to have elicited her enthusiasm but unsure about what she meant. He progressed boldly, knowing where the actor was headed from previous viewings and intent on pleasing Ling Ling.

"And now he's gonna go into the studio," he said.

"Yes, of course!" she exclaimed. "But this is the moment when we have to decide for him!"

How much he loved her! Just to hear her voice ring with the excitement of finding the scene that she considered the key to some enigma in life! He smiled and resisted the urge to touch her hair while she stared at the screen. He put his hand into the waistband of his underwear and thought about later, when they would make love. All of these sessions, after Ling Ling had raced home with a new disc, ended with her claiming to have a slightly better understanding of the world, and them having sex. Gao happily put up with it. With the remote control she froze the picture on the dancer's half-concealed face behind the curtain of her shiny hair.

"Here he has to find out whether she will be a blessing or a curse," Ling Ling explained.

Gao had fallen asleep, and the sudden movement in the room when she got up roused him. As soon as Ling Ling had disappeared into the tiny bathroom he leapt to his feet, peed into the kitchen sink, gargled with mouthwash, adjusted the blinds and air conditioner, turned off the TV, and set the alarm. He did these actions very rapidly, and succeeded in laying back on the bed as if he had not stirred a limb since she had gone into the bathroom. When she was close to the bed, with her hair pinned up and a towel wrapped around her, Gao leapt up and she faked being scared, and then they wrestled on the bed and made love.

*　*　*

On a chilly day in November they sat on the terrace of a snack bar in Pudong near the river, squinting at the skyline of the Bund through the afternoon haze. "The fact is that you think like Einstein," she said casually while picking pieces of mango from the ice cream she had ordered despite the cold. Gao gave her a questioning look.

"You think that time sometimes moves slowly, and sometimes fast, and that you can outrun it when you want," she continued.

"I don't really know much about Einstein," Gao responded apologetically.

"It's no problem," she said cheerfully. "Einstein thought that time moves at different speeds so you can catch up with whatever you've missed."

She leaned over and kissed him on the cheek.

"It's true," Gao responded, "I always think time with you moves too fast!"

The limestone buildings on the Bund faded from view quickly once the sun had set. Several barges plied the river before them, precariously balancing tall screens that flashed advertising images. The ice cream in Ling Ling's bowl had melted into a thin puddle. Gao would have to hurry to start his shift on time. He felt the familiar knot in his stomach because they would separate in a few moments.

"I don't have to go to school till second period tomorrow," she said as if she sensed his anxiety.

This meant that she would spend the night at his place, and he would be able to see her in the morning. He thought about the moment he would tiptoe into the apartment, dropping his clothes in the tiny kitchen and slipping into bed where she would be warm with sleep.

"That'll make tonight's shift pass quickly," he said happily.

"See," she added with a smile, "it proves that you believe time sometimes moves faster."

He smiled, a bit uncertain what to make of this thought. But on the boat, surrounded by a horde of noisy teenagers, she nestled up against him, slid a hand under his sweater and closed her eyes.

*　*　*

After the New Year's holiday, Ling Ling stayed with cousins in Nanjing for a few more days than planned. The following weekend she unexpectedly visited her hometown. When she saw Gao the following Tuesday she assured him that her parents were fine.

"I just had to take care of some things," she had said and briefly glanced at him. He had not asked for details.

"Leave it alone," his cousin advised on the phone that night. "If you ask a girl too many questions she'll think you don't trust her."

He had followed his cousin's counsel and instead of asking questions had bought her small presents. He laid out small bags with slices of dried pineapple and kiwi on the pillows. It looked like flowers had grown in the drab space, and he regretted not having bought more fruit, or a new comforter to replace the faded blue blankets that his landlord provided.

"I had to study for an exam," Ling Ling explained on the phone when he returned that night to find his apartment dark and empty, the bags of fruit unmoved and the air lifeless and stale. The weekend in Nanjing, another sudden trip to her hometown, then more and more nights where she had to study. This and that, another evening where he already felt sick to his stomach before he had turned the key and sensed with sudden certainty that his blustering presence alone would fill the room. Her explanations were always indisputable at the time.

"I'm sure she wants to get her teacher's license before settling down," Mother had reassured him on the phone. "It's important for a woman to have her own profession."

"But with your help I'll be able to buy a share of a taxi!" Gao responded, his pride hurt. "Then Ling Ling wouldn't have to work so much! And if I work weekends I'm sure we can make ends meet."

"Mother is right," Father added a minute later. "Women need their own jobs to contribute to society."

Gao was not convinced but did not want to pressure Ling Ling. She was under enough stress! Even the movie-watching sessions had become more serious, as if she was struggling to answer an urgent problem. But the sex was still great, and Gao was sure that things would return to normal. Be patient! he told himself when Ling Ling failed to show up another night. He practiced being patient during the day while driving through rush hour traffic, and managed not to curse under his breath when he got stuck behind a stalled bus, or some rich lady in a fancy western car that she didn't know how to drive.

One day without warning Ling Ling packed her clothes, towels, and a set of wrapped toothbrushes that Gao had bought in two bags and a rolling suitcase that she noisily pulled down the five flights of stairs on her way out. When she returned that night for what turned out to be her last visit she gingerly picked a few peaks from the miniature skyline of cosmetic containers on Gao's bathroom shelf, wrapped these in a hand towel and carried them out in a madras-printed plastic bag. Besides the scarred skyline of lotions and perfumes and a set of dishes, she left behind only a stack of DVDs.

In the first few days after Ling Ling's departure, Gao tried to ignore her absence the way he was ignoring a clanging noise with the belts of his Santana. Finally the car had stalled on an onramp to the Nanpu Bridge during rush hour. While it was in the shop, Gao found himself for three days at home without anything to do.

He sat on the vinyl two-seater and smoked the last of the cigarettes from Ling Ling's hometown to conjure up her image. He tried calling her over and over but she didn't respond. Finally he turned on the TV and fast-forwarded through the movies she had shown him. But he could not find the DVDs with the riding accident among the stack, nor the other scenes that had excited her so much. Perhaps Ling Ling had taken those movies? He put in disc after disc, careful to separate the scanned discs from the others. But soon there were stacks everywhere in the apartment, and the scenes from different movies began to blur. He muttered to himself to get it together, a glass of whisky in one hand and the remote in the other. If Ling Ling were here he would know which DVDs to watch, he thought after a few more glasses, and almost forgot that her leaving had prompted him to go through these viewings in the first place. When he hung his shirt over the lamp it fell over but Gao did not bother picking it up, and it stayed on the floor amidst the rest of his clothes, the discs, plastic bags and take-out containers.

Without Ling Ling the cramped apartment felt even smaller. He came home, drank whisky, and fell asleep sprawled across the thin mattress. When he woke up early in the morning the diffuse light poured past the limp curtains and pooled in the stagnant air, still full of smoke from the cigarettes of the previous night. His head hurt and he always found himself curled up on the edge of the bed as if his body had instinctively moved away from the side where Ling Ling had used to sleep. When it turned hot quite suddenly that spring he did not turn on the air conditioning but slept directly on the wooden floor next to the bed, as he had done when growing up. He stayed on the floor even when the temperatures came back down because sleeping on the bed made his head hurt more than the liquor did. The bed seemed senselessly large for the tiny room, and after a few weeks it was buried in clothes, shopping bags, and junk mail so that he would no longer have to see it when he got home.

He had heard Ling Ling's voice for the last time

when she called him during a shift.

"I dropped something at your house, Gao," he heard her voice while trying to keep the phone from his passenger's view.

"Ling Ling! How are you?" he had whispered hoarsely but she had already hung up. He dropped off the cab early that night and rushed home. Between the metal gate and his front door there was a paper envelope with a jade bracelet and two rings he had given her. He searched for a note but there was nothing.

* * *

For months Gao made it his business to snatch up moments of time and safeguard them for future use. Once there was a sufficient amount of moments, he mused during his shifts, he would find Ling Ling. He would present to her these moments snatched from the future and they would make up everything that they had lost. He clutched the steering wheel, abruptly changed lanes, and with bated breath raced across another intersection through blinking red lights.

During spring afternoons, between three and four, he sometimes stopped the cab in Hongqiao for lunch. He waved at a vendor to bring lunch to his car, and then devoured the hot food while scanning for traffic guards who could fine him for parking without a permit. Then, at exactly three minutes to four he dumped the plate in the gutter and slowly drove around the corner. This happened only every once in a while, and it was not as if he intentionally ended up in that part of Shanghai. He had to eat lunch, after all, and this spot was as good as any, and cheap!

Once he turned the corner he slowed the cab to a crawl directly in front of the school where Ling Ling worked. He waved away a few mothers who tried to get in his cab with their uniformed child in tow. "But your sign is on!" one woman insisted when her daughter had already climbed in the back.

"No service!" Gao barked while the woman cursed and pulled her kid out of the cab.

"I saved up all of these minutes for you," he would tell Ling Ling once they were back together. "Remember you told me once that I think time moves at different speeds?" he would explain. "It's true. So I caught all of the minutes by jumping ahead of time when I was supposed to wait, and let time just go by unused."

And she would understand right away. He would tell her how many minutes he had gathered for her. She would be beautiful! He would mention casually that he had watched all of the movies left at his house. Make it sound like their long separation had been nothing but a few days, and that her unexplained departure had not really torn a throbbing hole that no amount of whisky had been able to fill. He felt in his shirt pocket for the notebook that listed the minutes he had saved. He knew Ling Ling would marvel at the system he had devised in a larger notebook, with the cage-like grid in colored pencil that showed the day, location, and minutes he had snatched from the places where his cab had not yet been supposed to go.

"We had never had enough time, Gao," she would say and put her arms around him. "Thank you for saving up time for us."

Then Ling Ling would admit that leaving him had been a terrible mistake and beg him to take her back.

He would be magnanimous right away, not faulting her for anything. And they would go home and make love.

Gao waved away a young couple with the man wearing a t-shirt sparkling with rhinestones, and the girl all dolled up in pink. The man cursed loudly when Gao drove past. Gao scanned the students and parents spilling from the school gates. Perhaps today Ling Ling had to work late . . .

But no! There she was! Her hair seemed longer, but maybe that was just his imagination. She wore a shiny gray vest he did not know, with a puffy, stiff collar that made her look like a proud princess in full armor. She walked right past his cab next to two other teachers. He edged the cab closer toward the curb, forcing the stream of bicycles and scooters next to him to move toward the other side.

Ling Ling turned at the corner and Gao edged his cab through the intersection teeming with students and parents. Soon, he thought with his gaze locked on her head, soon he would offer her the time they had missed. Things would be good again. Now Ling Ling stood at the next crossing, her head turned toward the woman who was with her. Gao covered the side of his face with one hand in case she looked over. He was stopped two cars behind the light and when she waited for the walk sign he had a full long view of her. How beautiful she looked! But maybe also a bit sad? Perhaps she missed him! And perhaps she just hadn't been able to reach him? Gao felt for his phone but resisted the impulse, this time, to call her number. He had done it countless times before, had rung her while he had her locked in his sight from inside the cab. He remembered seeing her face cloud over when she glanced at the phone and how she had dropped it back in her purse, her face in a tight frown. It had stung badly, that look, and he had run his hands over his eyes in an effort to try to put it out his mind as quickly as possible.

Ling Ling crossed the street and Gao moved the cab along slowly without taking his eyes off her. A man suddenly appeared right in front of the cab, his hands on the hood and his eyes filled with fear. Gao stepped on the brake and stared at the man, not sure what had happened. Now the man backed away from the cab and shouted something.

"Pay attention!" Gao heard but his eyes were turned back to the sidewalk to look for Ling Ling. The man rapidly walked toward Gao's door. Gao nodded without looking at the man, his lips squeezed tight with embarrassment. Then the man suddenly stopped and padded his pockets, and turned and looked down to the curb as if he had dropped something. Gao jerked the cab forward so that the traffic closed behind and he would be out of the man's reach. He focused his attention back on the sidewalk to search for Ling Ling's face. He hit the steering wheel, his fright from having nearly hit the man turning to anger.

Gao bit his lip in frustration. Up ahead several people were lined up along the sidewalk, their eyes glued on the approaching traffic like herons at the edge of a stream. Yes! At the curb was Ling Ling! Gao slipped ahead of another cab. Today would be the day! Today he would offer to Ling Ling all the minutes he had snatched from the future. They would spend their evenings again watching Ling Ling's films, she would kiss him all over his face, and they would make love.

Gao drove past someone else and braked to a halt directly in front of Ling Ling. Quickly she stepped off the curb and reached for the door. He was overwhelmed with the prospect of seeing her again. When she glanced in through the window Gao caught her eye and tentatively lifted one hand from the steering wheel in greeting. Ling Ling jerked her hand back from the door as if it were scalding hot. She snapped her body up and stepped away fast, then almost ran the few steps to another cab that had pulled up behind Gao's. He watched in his rearview mirror when Ling Ling pointed her finger in the air in the direction of his cab. She got into the front seat and the cab pulled into traffic.

"Changning Lu, Jumen Lu," Gao heard and turned to discover that another passenger had slipped into his cab. He flipped on the meter as if by instinct, unsure of what to do next.

"You can go, *Shifu*," the passenger barked impatiently and clicked his tongue, as if Gao were a horse.

Up ahead, a light was just about to turn red. Gao could have squeezed across the intersection in the nick of time but instead he sharply braked to a stop. He sat there for several seconds, the corners of his mouth drawn down as if he were about to cry. A stream of bicycles, scooters, cars, buses and trucks filled the wide intersection before him, while above them a steady steam of traffic floated along the elevated highway. People ascended and came down the polished staircases and walkways that spanned the vast intersection, and then proceeded along the sidewalks lined with wrought-iron fences to keep them off the street.

Gao unbuckled his seat belt, took the key from the

ignition and got out of the cab. The passenger behind him looked up from his phone and emitted a sound of surprise. Gao threw the key over the meridian into traffic and walked straight ahead into the intersection. A truck swerved and barely avoided him, his driver leaning on the horn and cursing loudly. Gao stepped to the side and now walked on one of the white lines dividing the lanes of fast-moving traffic. The beeping horns, blaring radios and shouting drivers enveloped him as he changed from a walk to a trot, and then to a run, and then while Shanghai's traffic roared on in clouds of exhaust and glints of chrome, Gao disappeared from view.

ULRICH BAER

ABOUT THE AUTHOR

Ulrich Baer grew up in West Berlin, before moving to San Francisco after high school to work as a waiter. He received his B.A. at Harvard, where he was a varsity rower, and his Ph.D. in Comparative Literature at Yale. He teaches literature and photography at New York University, where he is Vice Provost for Arts, Humanities and Multicultural Affairs. In 2007, he lived for a period in Shanghai, and studied enough Mandarin to think that people understand him when he travels in China. He is the author of several books on photography, poetry and literature, editor of *110 Stories: New York Writes After September 11*, and editor and translator of Rainer Maria Rilke's letters. He lives in New York City and is the father of two children. *Beggar's Chicken* is his first book of fiction.